WHITEHAWK

Simon Nolan has published six novels under two names, many of which have sold in translation and in the USA. *As Good as it Gets*, his first novel, was published to great acclaim in 1999, followed by *The Vending Machine of Justice* (2001). He has also published short stories, one broadcast on BBC Radio 4. *Sheep* was filmed as *The Dark* (Sean Bean/Maria Bello, Impact Pictures, 2005) and *Methods of Confinement* was nominated for Novel of the Year by the British Fantasy Society. *As Good as it Gets* was listed by Julie Burchill as one of her top ten books.

Simon lives and works in Brighton, UK (Britain's hippest coastal city), and also writes as Simon Maginn.

ALSO BY SIMON NOLAN

AS GOOD AS IT GETS

'the funniest book I've read in aeons... Nolan is brilliant...'
Time Out

'exceptionally funny and realistic... Nolan's eye is perfect
for observation comedy...'
The Sunday Times

THE VENDING MACHINE OF JUSTICE

'brilliant black humour... a savage take on truth and justice,
with a real satirical bite that hasn't leaped out of the pages
since Evelyn Waugh...'
The Independent

'imagine Twelve Angry Men as a comedy set
by the seaside... fantastic.'
Time Out

www.simonmaginn.com

WHITEHAWK

SIMON NOLAN

REVENGE INK

British Library Cataloguing in Publication Data
A catalogue record for this book is available from the British Library

Revenge Ink
Unit 13 Newby Road, Hazel Grove, Stockport Cheshire, SK7 5DA, UK

www.revengeink.com

ISBN 978-0-9558078-7-9

Typeset in Paris by Patrick Lederfain
Printed in the EU by Pulsio, Ltd

For Hugh, as always

The Government's £40m campaign to encourage people to eat more fruit and vegetables has failed, with a decline in consumption in 2001-2002.

Independent, 25/4/03

O dark, dark, dark, amid the blaze of noon,
Irrecoverably dark, total Eclipse
Without all hope of day!

John Milton, *Samson Agonistes.*

1

'Jamie?' Mel said.

'Hmmm…'

'Would you say I demonstrated an evidence-based approach to decision-making?'

He moved his mouth away from her neck, and lay back on the sofa.

'Is it a trick question?'

She had what Jamie called her Wednesday face on, Wednesday being the day when The Guardian carried a thick, densely-printed social work appointments section. Sick of my job, her face said grimly as she flung the pages over, lips tightly compressed, not appreciated, not getting any younger, time to move on. This one looks good: see, working with proven bastards in extremely depressing circumstances in some toxic decimated sink-estate near Sunderland, for almost no money. No training, no support, and blame from all sides when it all goes wrong, which it invariably does. Applicants will, ideally, be utterly mad. Mel applied for many, but (thank God, Jamie thought) rarely got past the first interview stage. If she wanted to move from sunny, easy-going Brighton to Hell-near-

Middlesbrough to minister to the needs of drug-addled monsters that sold their children and smoked in Tesco, would he accompany her? Certainly, he thought soberly, I might prefer not to. As yet the question had not, quite, come up.

'Show me the ad' he said.

Thinking It Through

The project is looking to recruit qualified social workers, preferably experienced in family and child welfare, to act as Rationality Counsellors.Successful applicants will, after an initial training and evaluation phase, work intensively with one family over a three month period. The project aims to bring about a greater sense of order into lives that have suffered undesirable or disadvantageous social outcomes as a result of high levels of unreason.

Applicants must be able to demonstrate a flexible, holistic and multidisciplinary approach; must show a commitment to evidence-based decision making; and must have an awareness of ...

'Well, if you want me to be serious about it...' he said.

'No. I want you to say I do it. The rational thing and everything. I do don't I?'

'Course you do. In fact it was precisely that that first attracted me to you, oddly enough.' Jamie attempted to slide the Guardian away from her, but she caught it in time. 'I thought, finally after all this time I meet the kind of girl who really knows a thing or two about flexible, holistic...'

'Your brother said you fancied my tits, because I was wearing cashmere. He says you've got a thing about women and cashmere.'

'He's been saying things like that for decades. It doesn't make it true.'

'But is it true though?'

'Well yes it's true I suppose...'

'It's based right here,' Mel said plaintively. 'Brighton. Do you know how often jobs come up here?'

He pulled away, 'Not very often?'

'Whitehawk Estate, Brighton. See? It says.'

'Whitehawk eh?' Jamie said, and whistled softly. He knew, dimly, what Whitehawk meant, though like the majority of Brighton's residents he had never actually set foot in it and had no immediate plans to do so. No tourist ever went to Whitehawk either, and if they did they would obtain no usable pictures and, after dark, might not be entirely safe. There was no Royal Pavilion on the Whitehawk Estate, no B&Bs, no raffish Regency squares. Whitehawk was 1970's system-built deck-access low-rises; it was rain-swept concrete, petty crime, burned-out cars and random hostage dramas, always drug related. Fierce teenagers throw stones at the buses in Whitehawk. The children were feral and unsupervised (as, indeed, were the adults). Surrounded by a landfill site, a grim Victorian hospital (ex-workhouse) and a vast, sprawling crematorium complex, with the racecourse at the top, Whitehawk was entirely severed from the rest of Brighton, and Brighton seemed content for it to remain so. 'Lucky you,' Jamie said. 'Are you going to go for it?'

'Oh there's absolutely no point, they'll never have me. I haven't got...'

'OK. Don't go for it.'

'But it's perfect, look...'

'So sodding go for it then.'

'Oh fat lot of help you are,' she said, and tried to fold the paper up but only succeeded in tearing it. 'Go for it, don't go for it. Like it's that easy.'

'Sorry,' Jamie said, and got back to smoking. This was why he dreaded Guardian days. 'Sorry. There must be some kind of third way between going for it and not going for it that I've overlooked. You see, I haven't had the training...'

'In decision-making and that?'

'Exactly,' Jamie said, nuzzling her knee, whilst attempting to (accidentally) set fire to the paper, 'exactly sweetheart. Not like you.'

2

Mel arrived flushed and disorientated at the induction meeting. She had got lost three times inside the Rationality Unit building, which boasted an innovative room numbering system that she, somehow, completely failed to understand. There was a rack of leaflets on the imposing marble reception desk (available in a dazzling array of languages) which explained the system, but this too, sadly, she failed to master. The system, she read, was designed to accommodate the innate human tendency to regard objects to the right as more significant than objects to the left. Innumerable studies had shown that a system which prioritised right turns over left would increase efficiency by up to 26%, cut 'internal journey reiterations' by a third and generate a sense of 'intuitive engagement' with the building. (The leaflet, she noted, had itself won several awards.) She ferociously tore the pages trying to get some actual directions, but to no avail. The desk was unstaffed, and had the mournful look of a place that has been long untenanted.

She found the right room eventually, but more by luck than judgement. It was a large basement meeting room with chairs arranged in lines in front of a central raised podium. There were sixty or so other applicants seated in the conference room with expensive-looking brochures set out in front of them. Thinking It Through. Nervously, Mel flipped the pages. The background. The issues. The solution. Lots of white space and pictures of belligerent men and end-of-their-rope women being interviewed by smiling professionals in reassuringly informal clothes. A scrupulous balance of ethnicity and disability, gender and age. Trials in other countries: the Danish experience, the Dutch. Graphs and flow charts and tables of figures.

The group were awaiting their leader.

'Well whatever this is about it's got to be better than what I'm doing at the moment,' said a slightly rumpled-looking woman next to Mel. Her glasses were loose on her nose and her shoes seemed to belong to some other outfit altogether.

'Oh?'

'Mental health. Adolescents. Jesus. If I have to listen to one more fucking poem…'

Mel was startled more by the sentiment than the profanity. She attempted a full, disarming smile.

'Still, this all looks very interesting doesn't it?'

'It's all the same bollocks,' the woman said and started to draw giant phalluses on the pictures in the brochure. Mel curled her lip. Professional cynicism. She just didn't like it. If you didn't want to help people, then what were you doing in social services? Hm?

Mel tried to indicate her disapproval by burying herself in the glossy booklet. She read a sentence containing the words 'disadvantageous cognitive matrices' four times, then glanced at the pictures on the facing page. Underneath the caption 'Client families undergo regular monitoring' was a picture of the back of a man's head and part of a woman's pony tail – just from their necks you knew they were trouble, these two; his uncomprehending, self-righteous and truculent, hers tilted in a way that was strongly suggestive of some kind of subnormality. Monstrously strong sense of entitlement, much unfocused rage. Facing them was a pretty Asian woman with a laptop and an encouraging smile. She had quite exceptionally beautiful nails, Mel was noting, when the door opened, and all faces turned. A striking young woman came in, exuding confidence from every deodorised pore. Even her briefcase exuded it, Mel thought, with an absent tug of longing. The briefcase carried a discreet black and white logo, RU.

'OK. Everyone?' she said, her voice full of projection and a kind of bullying good humour. 'My name is Eleni, and I will be facilitating today's induction. OK?'

No one was prepared to object to this ugly statement. Mel's neighbour picked aggressively at her nails. Mel tried to look intelligent. Eleni got the slides organised, and they were off.

'Now I'd like to kick off with some figures, if that's OK with everyone. For instance...' and here she clicked on her first slide: a fire engine with firemen standing around it.

'Facts: 8% of all call outs to the Fire Brigade are hoaxes. Almost 80% of admissions to accident and emergency departments are the direct result of poor decision making with regard to alcohol. 4 out of 5 new admittances to British jails test positive for heroin or crack cocaine. One in five British adults cannot read the instructions on a medicine bottle or use the Yellow Pages. Doctors estimate that somewhere between 85 and 90% of all surgery visits are based on misunderstanding, delusion or mistaken fact. A study in Truro showed that 15% of adult job-seekers answered 'correct' to the statement: 'if you give a monkey a typewriter he will write Hamlet.' A recent survey showed that three out of ten British sixteen year olds thought that aliens regularly visit the earth: two of the three would go on to say that this had been 'proved beyond any doubt' and that the government was involved in a conspiracy to hide the truth. This same group demonstrated a profound systematic misunderstanding of the ordinary laws of chance. The writer David Icke has made a career worldwide from books explaining that the world is, in fact, ruled by giant lizards.

'Now, whilst none of these beliefs and behaviours may, themselves, be dangerous, the total cost to British society of the sum of all unreasonable, irrational or simply mistaken beliefs and the behaviours associated with them has been estimated to be between £12.2 and £18.7 billion annually. This has recently been characterised as the 'stupidity levy', or less politely, 'idiot charge'.

'This pilot project, funded jointly by the Rationality Unit, The Office of the Deputy Prime Minister, The Department for Work and Pensions and the EUCRDF, is unique in British society.

'Take the hoax fire brigade call-outs, for example. One in twelve calls. And the service is, of course, obliged to attend each one. What this means is that the fire service is wasting one in twelve of its hours. If the average annual pay for a fire-fighter is £21,000, that means that £1750 pounds of that is simply dissipated. One in twelve...'

Yes, I think we've probably got the point now, Mel thought. One in twelve. Right.

'...and of course every call-out has a fixed cost, in terms of personnel, equipment, IT backup... Merely to deploy a single appliance costs almost ...'

A new slide, with a number in pounds on it in huge red figures and an exclamation mark.

'This is a Fire Service estimate of the total annual cost of hoax call-outs in Britain every year.' She allowed the figure, which was indeed impressive, to speak for itself for a moment.

'So why is this the case? Why, for heaven's sake, is this happening?'

She scanned the room, where no one was keen to be picked on to answer.

'I mean, is it enough to say, oh well, the kids are bored, they've got no facilities, they're just hanging around getting into trouble, build them a skateboard park and an amateurish mural in 'graffiti' style and that'll sort them out? Which has, of course, been the traditional approach to the problem? And what does that do for the adults?' Again, no takers for an answer. The woman next to Mel stirred.

'They could be encouraged to write poems about it,' she said, to scattered sniggers round the room. Suddenly everyone was back in double geography again.

'Yes, yes, that's an interesting suggestion,' said Eleni. 'And that also is very much part of the approach that's been the consensus over the last, let's say, fifty years. Understand, support, invest, hope. Build stable communities, all that. But the figures,' and here she put her hand on a copy of the report, 'the new figures just don't bear that out that as a solution. You will see that in areas where additional support of this type has been put into place, the incidence of, for instance, hoax fire brigade call-outs has not always been reduced. In some cases it has actually gone up. The evidence suggests that this method, which has been described as the Delinquency Reward Model, is simply failing to deliver results. What we see instead is the increased use of Anti-Social Behaviour Orders and curfews and all the rest of it. And ultimately, jail, at appalling cost to the taxpayer and with no discernible benefit either to the offender or their community on release.

'You see, what this approach fails entirely to address is the fact that calling out a fire engine when there's no fire is simply an irrational act. Not only does it use resources wastefully, but it also endangers your own safety, by stretching the available services beyond their limit. Now this is actually counter to your own self-interest, since you or your family may well be in need of precisely that facility yourself. It is not anti-social so much as anti-reasonable. It indicates what a recent US study identified as a 'willed cognitive deficit', a state in which decisions are made with no reference to evaluative or analytical processes. It is this that the Thinking It Through project is about.'

A new slide: a single question mark.

'What is being attempted here is something quite new. It is an approach in which undesirable behaviours are seen, not as the result of deprivation or lack of opportunity and so on, in other words not as the product of a faulty social system, but as the product of faulty reasoning. What this project does is engage, confront and attempt to overcome the belief and logic systems which are bringing these behaviours about. Typically client families will have clusters, or matrices, of such beliefs, which can be only be dismantled with great patience and skill. There will often also be what the Copenhagen Protocol identifies as 'master themes', deep structures of belief around which whole behaviours can be built, and 'life themes', fundamental attitudes about the self and the state, about entitlement, victimhood, often used to defend the acquisition of habits of dependency...'

Mel found that, somehow or other, she had stopped listening.

'You'll be familiar with the principles of Cognitive Behaviour Therapy, of course..?' Eleni said suddenly, looking expectantly round the room and getting very little response, '...well this is, if you like, the next step. Instead of merely attempting to bring about change in an individual psyche, we are trying to harness those techniques and insights in the service of a wider social agenda. It is, in effect, nothing less than a programme for changing the ways people think. About themselves, yes, but also about the society they live in. Changing minds. Literally.' Great big smile, all around the room. There was a slightly stunned silence.

'Thought police,' someone at the back of the room muttered, and Eleni smiled aggressively over at him.

'Ah, but the difference here is that the changes are agreed and negotiated. There's no compulsion. All parties are working in partnership towards agreed goals. Families either volunteer for the programme or are selected for it by referral with their consent. What's more, the scheme allows for rewards for behavioural and conceptual change. There is a 'points' system, and points can be redeemed for cash at the end of the programme. I don't think Mr. Kubrick would have imagined anything quite like that…' she said, still smiling at everyone.

'Orwell. It's New Labour bollocks,' said the woman next to Mel, who now wished she was sitting further away from her. 'They'll drop it in six months and have some other bollocks instead.'

'Bollocks in Partnership,' came a voice from another part of the room.

'New Community Bollocks Partnership Initiative.'

Eleni raised an eyebrow thus effortlessly quelling the rebellion.

'If there is any political agenda here,' she intoned almost caressingly, 'it is an agenda that we can surely all share, both as citizens and as taxpayers ourselves. If we can bring about real and lasting change in the client group, we will, at a stroke, cut many of the costs associated with some of the most resource-wasteful people and families in society. The savings will benefit everyone. Politics is about change. We shouldn't be afraid of that. In a way, Thinking It Through is really just an extension of the existing Continuing Education movement, except that, instead of teaching art history or modern languages or whatever, it teaches, and rewards, what might most simply be described as reasonable behaviour. To adults, and to their children. Nothing more, nothing less. Now I'd like us all to watch a video, which was made under the guidance of the European Union Community Regeneration and Development Fund which presents what has been called The Copenhagen Model. Denmark was the first European Union country to attempt a programme of this sort. Would someone mind dimming the lights please…?'

The video was presented by an earnest young European called Luub Flummers, whose job title took two lines of text (and parenthesis) to express fully. Establishing shots of tourist Copenhagen, Tivoli Gardens, tall glasses of beer; then a speeded up segment taking us to a somewhat less attractive location, a 1970's built sink estate halfway out to the airport, seemingly made out of streaky concrete and damp. Here we saw a specialist adviser talking about the shiny billions of Euros allocated to the desperate place. His English was fluent and beautiful, except that he was inclined to emphasise syllables somewhat randomly. Regeneration, for instance, came out 're-GEN-ertion', development was 'dev-LOPE-ment.' (Mel sensed sniggers coming from next to her and diligently blanked them out.) Scary local youths were interviewed, in Danish with subtitles, then their no less terrifying parents. News footage of some kind of straggling, incoherent riot, the police seemingly much better equipped for, and more strongly motivated against this kind of thing than their British counterparts, Mel thought. Lingering shots of things burned out and smashed in and generally trashed, including a suspiciously new-looking Youth Centre. Broken computers. Sad music.

It switched to animated graphs and figures, all of which appeared to be rising at an alarming rate. Mel felt her attention wandering. Academics speaking to camera in bland offices with good views.

Next, a group of what Mel was able to recognise instantly as social workers (she could tell by their lustreless hair and air of patient martyrdom). They were sitting in a classroom; the whiteboard behind them was full of words in Danish and many exclamation marks. We focus in on one of them, a young woman in a distinctive blue jacket. Then she is seen interviewing a couple of hard-case adults. The season abruptly changes from spring to summer. Much earnest talk with a family, much sweat-stained polyester, around various laminate tables.

At first the clients were hostile, arms crossed, 'why-should-we?' looks on their faces. But as the weeks passed, the expressions softened. After a while there was even a shot of a woman weeping – quite possibly with gratitude – on the social worker's shoulder. A manly handshake from the daddy, banter with the children.

Then a group discussion: the family were having a debate! They were discussing GM manipulation of crops with the social worker, but the astonishing thing was (and subtitles made this wholly explicit) that no one was shouting at anyone or throwing anything, they were listening to each other's opinions, discussing the reliability of sources – they were behaving rationally. It was working.

Now look: daddy was chairing a local community association meeting. He was making a speech! He'd made a joke! Everyone loved and cherished him.

A scene (presumably staged for the cameras), in which the woman of the family grandly signed off from her lifetime of benefit fraud and pointless petty criminality, and was then seen striding, neatly suited, into a lovely glass office to begin her rewarding new work life. More whizzy graphics, but now the graphs were all pointing downwards. Budgets were being slashed, negative attitudes were being eroded, and the outcome (the final shot told you) was a happy, prosperous and rational citizenry, standing on their own two sturdy Danish feet and in every way a credit to their regenerated new communities, standing foursquare on their own doorsteps, waving. One final figure: the total saving, in Euros, for the first year of the scheme. A great big whopping number. A flurry of logos from various EU funding bodies, a final serene wave of the blue flag with stars...

The lights came back on again.

'God. Maybe adolescents aren't so bad after all,' Mel's friend muttered. 'At least they grow out of it. Well some of them do.'

'Now,' Eleni said, smiling happily round the room. 'I'm sure you'll have some questions?'

3

Mel and Jamie were on the sofa having a dummy run for her second round interview the next day. They were also drinking, and Jamie was managing to do both of those things and smoke what he'd started calling ca-*nar*-bis, and watch Newsnight, all at the same time. Multi-skilling or what, he thought.

'Right. So, candidate. The panel would be grateful if you would give us your understanding of some of the philosophical and methodological underpinnings...' he said, sternly.

'OK I know this one.' She put her glass down by the sofa and immediately kicked it over. She needed both hands free, it seemed, for this question; plus maybe she just needed to spill. 'Right. Conceptual Disability Model presupposes an analogy with other disabilities, suggesting that material support and special, er, arrangements can be utilised to, er, to, you know...'

'You don't know do you.'

'No I do. Hold on. Cognitive Disability...'

'Conceptual...'

'Right, Conceptual Deficiency Model...'

'Disability...'

'That's right, whereas, whereaaaas, what did you say? The other one?'

'Cog-ni-tive…'

'Right. Got it. OK. Cognitive Deficit Model recognises specific behaviours in the context of – in the co-o-o-n-text – o-o-o-o-f…'

'Mel. Please. You quite obviously know nothing whatsoever about any of this…'

'No I do, Jamie, actually, if you'd let me finish please. Wait. It's – you see the difference is that one of them is old and bad and the other one's American.'

'That's the difference is it?'

'Essentially. Yes.'

'In layman's terms?'

'Exactly. Ask me another. Anything you like.'

'No, sounds like you've pretty much got everything covered.'

He went to get the cloth from the kitchen. He anticipated a good deal more wine spilling before bed.

'OK, now ask me what qualities I think I would bring to the job. Go on,' she shouted in to him.

'Desperation?' he muttered darkly. He knew her qualities by now. God forbid anyone else should have to as well.

4

When Mel opened the letter saying she'd got the job, she thought it said she hadn't. She had to have it read to her by Jamie, after which she rubbed it over her body and danced about singing 'I'm too sexy for my job,' until he tried to stuff it into her mouth.

This time she only got lost twice in the Rationality Unit HQ, and managed to find her supervisor's room by a process combining her 'intuitive engagement' with the building with a backup strategy of asking everyone she met on her way. No one was certain, but there was a growing consensus that she needed to find floor Delta, quarter PX.

Richard, the supervisor, greeted her warmly and was solicitous about her journey. Had she found the place alright, any difficulties? No, none at all, Mel said proudly. Well, you know.

'Now, my first priority, Mel, is to get your responses to everything so far. The induction, the building, and how you feel your expectations have so far been met, or not met. There's a form here, so if you wouldn't mind…'

The form was lengthy and detailed, and required her to tick on a scale of one to seven how 'satisfied' or 'dissatisfied' she was with various aspects of the operation. She went for safety, scattering 3's and 4's over the form with abandon.

While she was doing this, Richard was rummaging about in a filing cabinet. He returned to the desk with a set of overstuffed ring binders. Big fat white horrible ones. There was one called Objectives, one called Protocols, and a thinner one called Methodologies. Richard solemnly handed them over, and Mel tried to look as if she couldn't wait to get stuck in to them. He took some trouble to explain exactly what Mel's position was with regard to her fellow workers at the Practice. Her status was slightly odd in that she was funded differently, and whilst expected, of course, to participate fully as a team member, would be assessed, supervised and monitored by him, here, at the Rationality Unit HQ. OK? Mel nodded keenly. The Rationality Unit are also available for any further supervision you might need, or wish for, he added, and Mel noticed the little black and white RU logo on an enamel badge on his lapel. Great, she said. Whatever. There were some other files as well, all either marked "Medcrupp" or "Ireland" or "Medcrupp /Ireland", that were duly handed over. Her first family. Her mission. Her problem for the next three months. First supervision session would be in two weeks time. And good luck. Too skinny, she thought, this Richard, and too sodding young, frankly. And stop twinkling at me will you?

The files made it all seem real. She found herself bracing something, girding something; she felt a tremulous slippery knot deep in her belly. OK, she thought, as she absently shoved the files under the passenger seat alongside sandwich wrappers and a plastic bag full of tools belonging to Jamie. She took some deep breaths. Please make me not fail utterly and humiliatingly, she intoned as she put her seatbelt on. Please let me not have to look like a total twat. Handbrake. And please don't make me have to go back to Child and Family, ever, ever, ever, Amen. OK? Blow on your thumbs three times and it'll come true.

After all, how hard could it be?

5

On her last day at Child and Family Welfare she got a card signed by everyone and a stuffed baby seal with gooey eyes and a 'We'll miss you!' card hung round its neck. They all went to the pub at lunchtime and Paddy, the one Mel was most pleased to be finally getting some distance from, overdid his goodbye kiss a bit.

'I wish you weren't leaving,' he said, prolonging the hug quite shamelessly and managing to hold on to her in a way that was simultaneously too hesitant and too emphatic at the same time. Needy. Wet-mouthed. Mel delicately extricated herself. He was a big bear of a man, bearded, straggly, unfinished-looking.

'Ah well. Pastures new,' she said, patting him on the shoulder in a comradely kind of way. She had been saying this, or variants on it, for a good few weeks now. 'And we can still keep in touch.' (That also. As if.)

'Definitely,' Paddy said, all liquid eyes like the baby seal, and Mel tried not to notice that he had dandruff actually in his eyebrows and that the rough patch on the back of his neck looked like it was shedding again. 'Definitely.' In touch. Just not physically, Mel added internally.

Mel had been at Child and Family Welfare for nearly three years now. Her first real full-time job, her first office. And while she wasn't prepared to say it had all been some kind of ghastly, nightmarish mistake – the kind it could easily take her the rest of her life to recover from – it had, certainly, been a steep learning curve. It had quickly, for instance, got into her language: everyone in the office used tired governmental phrases like 'steep learning curve', but with a satirical twist in the voice, cod-American or cod-newsreader or – everyone's favourite – cod-Tony Blair. You know, er... Everyone was an impressionist. Mel found herself doing it all the time. Her particular speciality was saying 'literally think the unthinkable' in Prince Charles.

The client group – the fierce, despairing single mothers; the drunk fathers full of incoherent, retributive rage against the mothers; and the cynical, wary children caught up in it all – presented what Mel's Practice Manager blandly described as 'a broad spectrum of challenges'. The idea was that you managed to do something about it all before the children started getting knocked about or worse. But the children just kept on getting knocked about, and worse, and Mel had over the last six months come increasingly to feel as if she was merely a witness to it all. No amount of support would ever hold these people up, she thought in her dark moments; you could support them with high-tensile carbon-fibre hawsers designed by leading television architects and they would still fall down.

But that was defeatist talk, of course, Daily Mail talk, and not greatly appreciated round here, where measured optimism about the human condition was the house style. Because, after all, if you didn't believe you could do something about it, then what were you doing in social work at all? It was a question which, somehow, came up quite often.

And it was a good and interesting question, Mel thought, as she watched Paddy stroking the grey nylon fur of the baby seal in an absent, melancholy way. A question which fully deserved an answer. Oh yes.

But finally, at last, she was moving on. Praise Jesus. A new job. Not only a new job, but actually a new kind of job, a pilot scheme (she liked the sound of the words) which, if successful, would be rolled out (sounds good too) as part of a national strategy. A radical new approach.

'Nice brochure,' Jamie had said when the application pack had arrived, and subjected it to a long, slow, disdainful scrutiny. 'Must have cost a bit. Let's see now. Conceptual disability. Right. Do they send their own team to the Paralympics, the conceptually disabled?'

'Jamie…'

'Mel, people don't do things because they're conceptually disabled, they do things because they feel like it and they get something out of it. And because they're wankers. Half of them.'

'What, exactly half? Have you got figures from Denmark…?'

'Oh you can prove anything with figures from Denmark. Everything's true in bloody Denmark. Just don't try living there, that's all.'

'I see. Any other helpful comments?'

'The Enlightenment dream, armies of rationalist missionaries dispersing throughout the gibbering populace, spreading the gospel of scepticism and critical thinking.'

Jamie was reaching the end of his English degree – dissertation on pessimism in the English novel of ideas, Wells, Huxley, C.P. Snow – and was somewhat inclined to speak in paragraphs.

He was not yet officially (six months after the momentous first night together) living with Mel – he maintained a dim, dank room in a shared house up Elm Grove way – but hers was (much) nicer, and he spent many of his days here. His position was ambiguous, particularly as regard to share of bills. When Mel wasn't there he would creep about the flat, with the blinds drawn, feeling like a burglar. Or, more exactly, like a stalker suddenly given complete and uninterrupted access to his target's domain. He knew the current position of every object in the flat probably better than Mel did. He could worry for whole days at a time about a misplaced tissue box on her dressing table.

In between shifts collecting glasses at the Gala bingo, he was currently supposed to be talking himself – and his supervising tutor – into the master's thesis that would keep him safely away from having to get a proper job for the next two years, his labours ceaselessly interrupted by dope smoking and masturbation. Graham Greene: Towards a Hermeneutics of Despair. Snappy title huh? And wasn't Graham Greene perhaps rather a well-worn seam? His tutor was also inclined to quibble about the word 'hermeneutics', urging more methodological clarity and inviting Jamie to consider the hermeneutical as opposed to the merely exegetical. Yes? Jamie looked at him blankly. His tutor had a fixed questioning smile which did little to disguise his opinions, on Jamie in particular and on post-grad proposals in general, which ranged from genial incredulity to amused dismay.

Jamie had a video of the Boulting Brothers' film of Greene's Brighton Rock which he would sometimes find himself watching several times in a day. He knew much of the dialogue by heart and would sit, half-dressed, curtains drawn, joint smouldering in his fist, as he intoned, 'As Mephistopheles said to Faust, why this is hell, nor are we out of it'. Research, he told himself, ironically. He would be evasive and dishevelled sometimes when Mel came home.

He had begun to feel obscurely resentful about the whole idea of a Master's thesis, even though it was he who was initiating it. No one, after all, was exactly banging on the door pleading for another academic essay on Graham Greene, now were they? He imagined desperate men arguing fiercely with him in a shadowy basement. You're our only hope now, Kurwen. If this Graham Greene thing doesn't happen, then it's all over for us...

The whole idea was starting to seem like a nightmare. And the only way to fund it would be even more shifts at the Gala bingo. Two fat ladies seventy four.

He blew a long and thoughtful line of smoke. 'Anyway, I'm all for it if it keeps the costs down, and those scumbags cost plenty.'

'Sorry, which scumbags is it we're talking about now?' Mel said, faking confusion.

'You know very well. Your beloved client group. Policing, criminal justice, drug crime, drug rehabilitation, health, welfare, special bloody needs – which they've all got in spades, obviously – jail, probation, detox, *re*tox, re-offending, rehabilitation... As long as it's untreatable and expensive to deal with, and they don't actually have to pay for anything, they've got it, because...'

'Because...'

'...of a potentially lethal combination of chicken nuggets, raw polyester and poor impulse control...'

'And your solution would be...?'

'Camps. Well obviously. On the Isle of fucking Wight. How else do you think you're going to turn around all those generations of strategic underachievement?'

'I thought you already had the geriatrics living on the Isle of Wight.'

'What do they care? They don't know where they are half the time anyway.'

'Right.'

'And then your precious client group will be allowed out when they can tell you the meaning of the term 'public expenditure'. Maybe that's a concept they could be a bit less disabled about…'

'Jamie, do you think you really are a life partner for me, or just some kind of erotic plaything?'

'Tell me the options again,' he said, and she rolled over onto the remote and (accidentally) switched Newsnight off.

'You're not concentrating,' she said after ten minutes and Jamie pulled his hand away and grunted. He'd had what he described as 'a bit of a mad session' earlier on, and had pretty much drained his tank, as he chose to put it.

'Can't you fake it?'

He thought not, on balance, probably. He'd gone into sudden catastrophic zinc depletion syndrome, he said. He'd need props. He might even need a government initiative…

'Ah well,' she said, and put Newsnight back on. She had other things to think about anyway. Tomorrow she would meet them: the client family.

6

Mel's first meeting with the Medcrupp/Irelands and their Extended Network Group was in a conference suite at the Mentorn Hotel, a large rectangular room with the table taken out, a pay bar nearby, and an enviable supply of fire exits. Mel peered at the assembly through a crack in the doors and, despite all the briefings, was still momentarily overwhelmed by the sheer scale of them, not only the numbers (eight adults and an uncountable number of children), and not merely by their physical stature (these were big adults, big children,) but by the intensity of the field they emanated. The room was hot and itchy with them. Pale wood chairs with plum-coloured seats were arranged round the walls in two wide semicircles. The women were fierce, pulling mercilessly on cigarettes; the men dense, secret, brooding; the children pushing their luck. Crisp bags and juice cartons and ashtrays. Mel had a moment of incapacitating terror and had to physically force herself to push open the door and smile. Rule number one; show no fear.

'OK. Everyone?'

Heads turned in her direction, arguments were hurriedly shelved, children intimidated until they resentfully settled, belongings stuffed into pockets and under seats. She took a meanly-padded chair in the middle of one of the semicircles, arranged her papers, took a breath, and stood.

'OK! First I'd like to welcome everybody and say thank you for coming.'

'Had no choice did we?' A voice from her far left. She smiled tightly. No point in getting involved in any discussion yet.

'It's lovely to see you all in the flesh, after just reading your names. It'll take me a while to sort out exactly who's who, so you'll have to bear with me!'

Blank faces, faces which, if they knew the meaning of 'to bear with someone' were certainly not about to start doing it here. Why should they? Murmured threats to children.

'But I thought I'd kick off today by saying a few words about why we're all here and what we all hope to achieve over the course of the meeting.'

'Because we're not all there,' came the voice from the far end, an older man. Mel smiled encouragingly at him.

'Sorry, er...?'

'Kenneth love. Ken. That's why we're all here. Because we're not all there.'

Mel tried not to panic or freeze, but she simply couldn't understand a word he was saying. Some essential part of her comprehension equipment had suffered a component failure, and she was standing there, blank as a fish, faces all turned her way, even the fractious children sensing that there might be something worth seeing here now. Would she cry?

'Sorry, are there any of us missing?' she said, casting round the room and trying to remember how many there should be. There seemed to be thousands.

'Yeah I am. Carry on love. Don't mind me,' Kenneth said, and whispered something to a bearded adult beside him, who sniggered. An ugly, complicit, hostile sound. Plough on.

'So. Now. My name is Mel, I'm twenty-four years old, and I'm a qualified social worker. This is a new job for me, so we'll all be learning together, as we go. I'm sure you know the basic outline of the scheme, but I'd like to go over a few things, to set minds at rest.

'First of all, I'm not here to spy on you, or tell tales, or anything like that. That's got nothing to do with my job. I'm here to observe. To start with anyway. I just want to get a good look at you, see how everything's going, talk to you, find out as much about you as I can, what you think, what you feel, what you want. That's really it. To start with anyway.'

'And then what?'

'Well, after the initial evaluation phase…' (wrong register) '…after the first few weeks when I've got the hang of you a bit, then we go on to discuss ways in which we can start changing anything that you're not happy about. In your lives.'

'How you going to do that then? Got a magic wand have you?' Sniggering.

'Well really by talking to you, listening to you, and maybe suggesting the odd thing you might not have thought of…' (sell it to them. Tell them about the money) '… and then any changes that do occur, if they're broadly in line with project desiderata… I mean, if we can all agree that the changes are for the best, for you, then what we do is to award points.'

'Points.'

'That's right. Like a loyalty card. You know the kind of thing I mean? And then at the end we add up all the points and convert them to a single, one-off tax-free payment.'

A stirring round the room.

'What if we don't get no points?'

'Oh but you will. You'll see. That's what I'm here for,' she said, and smiled broadly around, inviting confidence: a sea of faces took in her young, eager, inexperienced features. The sound of judgements being reserved.

'You on commission?'

'Not exactly. It'll all be much clearer as we go on. But that's the outline of the scheme. Now you're going to be seeing quite a lot of me over the next few months I'm afraid, I'll be with you a couple of times a week, and I'll be sleeping over a few nights as well. You'll have had the details of how that's all going to work, reimbursement for any expenses and so on...'

'How much money?'

This was Kenneth again, sitting back, arms folded sceptically across chest. A nearby woman tried to shush him, but he was undeterred.

'It's all in your briefing pack, which I'll give you to take away at the end of the meeting. And I'll be happy to take any questions you might have then as well...'

'Like, how much money?'

She paused.

'I think it would be a mistake to focus too much on that aspect of the scheme at this point...' Stirrings of discontent. A babe in arms wailed briefly and was ruthlessly placated. 'Let's just say that we think it's important to offer incentives, and that the incentives will be well worth your trouble having.'

'Have you got it, like, on you?' said a man half way down, and Mel again felt a freeze of panic about the whole idea. She found herself noting again the many fire exits.

'The money you mean? No no, that'll all be sorted out at the end of the scheme.'

'What about an advance? For good behaviour?'

'The scheme doesn't actually allow for... I think it would be a mistake to focus too narrowly on...'

She'd lost them, there was a ripple of muttering and more

sniggering from the far end. They'd been joking. Of course. Hadn't they?

'You see, really, as you're probably well aware, the rewards of the scheme are not financial ones. Well there are financial rewards, as I've said, but actually what we're all hoping is that you'll gain something much more valuable than money out of it.'

Sceptical looks. Yeah right.

'So how come we get the money then? What's that, a bribe?'

'No no no no no.' (Yes.) 'No, you see, what we hope is that we're going to be able to help you in all kinds of ways. Make your lives easier. Help you out with things that are perhaps holding you back from realising your full potential…'

'Like having no money…'

'But the scheme is not primarily about money,' Mel said, unable to keep the exasperation out of her voice. The temperature of the room abruptly dropped ten degrees. Her heart hammered in her chest. She felt sweat gather around her knees. 'I have to say again, we're looking for families who are open to the possibility of making changes in their lives. It's about much more than money.' Scattered murmurs. Pause.

'But there is…''Yes.

There is a cash incentive. Yes. OK? Now are there any questions on any other subjects?'

Nothing for a moment. Mel found herself meeting the nervous, evasive eye of a girl, about fourteen or fifteen, and smiled again. Second rule: keep smiling.

'How old did you say you are? Sorry I've forgotten your name…' This was from a big woman in Adidas sweats with such ferociously scraped back hair that her face looked as if it might crack open at any minute. Big hoop earrings. She seemed, Mel thought distantly, drugged.

'Mel. I'm twenty-four.'

'Twenty-four. You see, I was only wondering, and I'm not being funny or anything, but some of us here are a bit older than that. I mean I'm forty-three.' Muffled sniggering. 'Reason I mention it, I just wonder what you've got to offer people who are that bit older than you…'

'… and wiser.'

Mel took a breath. Perfectly reasonable question.

'Yes. You see, it's not about me knowing better than you. I'm not here to, you know, pass judgement on you. What we'd like is for you to think of me as a kind of resource. You can say anything to me, and if I can help I will, and if I can't, well I can't. And I've got a whole team behind me to back me up, if you need any specialist help with anything. I'm not, I mean no one's suggesting that I've, that we've got an answer for everything. But we're here to try. That's all we can do. Yes, at the far end…?'

'Are you married love?' Kenneth again.

'No, Mr…'

'Kenneth love. Ken.'

'No Ken, I'm not…'

'Courting?'

'Yes.'

'Name of…?'

'Jamie. He's called Jamie.'

'Jamie what?'

'Kurwen. Is it important?'

'Nice boy?'

She smiled, almost laughed, with surprise. 'Yes. He is.'

'Kiddies?'

Smile. 'No, not so far…'

'Problems?'

'Sorry?'

'I said, are you having problems? In that department?'

Pause. Sound of a crisp bag being ground into a nylon carpet tile.

'No. Of course not.'

'Any plans?'

'Maybe. Not any time soon.'

'Fair enough. Just checking.'

Mel had the pounding sensation of having failed a test, the meaning of which was unclear to her. She suddenly felt extremely dehydrated. The skinny listless girl met her eye again and, disconcertingly, winked in a way that Mel failed to understand. She was wearing rather a lot of ruby red blusher, Mel noted. 'You're going to get to know me pretty well over the next few weeks, so we could maybe hold off any more questions about me until…'

'What music do you like?' This was the nervous girl, her voice a tired ghost of a sound. She twined a strand of black hair as she spoke. Mel sighed.

'Oh I don't know. All sorts.'

'But not classical?'

'Not really.' That, apparently, put her mind at rest. Another test, this time Mel had passed. But what did any of it mean? Sweat tickled her back. She patted her sides.

'Right, well if there are no more questions for the moment I thought we might…?'

'Just one more love…' That voice again. Ken. Kenneth. She steeled herself. Smiled. The room was full of eyes.

'Yes. Ken?'

'Say you had to get rid of a body part.'

'…sorry, I…?'

'A body part. Say you'd cut someone. Taken a trophy. But you had to hide it. Where do you put it?' He sat back, arms still folded, and she saw a fat wet tongue come out and lick his bristly lips.

Third rule; don't run. Ever.

'Well Ken, I'm not sure that's…' Silence. The hum of air conditioning. The sound of glasses tinkling from a faraway bar. Eyes. 'Right, well if that's everything…'

'Just one more.'

'Well, OK, Ken, but…'

He made her wait. Deadpan.

'Yeah last one love: can you cook?'

7

Baseline Assessments.

Kui/Varney Diagnostic Rationality Questionnaire. Conducted by M. Banff, May 17.

Kenneth Medcrupp, (49), DOB: 10/4/54
'OK Mr Medcrupp.'
'Kenneth, love.'
'Kenneth. Now I'm going to read you out a statement and all I want you to do is to listen, and then say 'true' if you think it's true, and 'false' if you think it's false. OK?'
'Right.'
'Socrates was a man. All men are mortal. Therefore Socrates was mortal.'
'What's mortal?'
'Means you're going to die.'
'False.'
'You think that's false?'
'No I was lying.'
'Why?'
'I thought that was the whole point, to see if you could tell if I was lying or not.'

'No, as we went through many times at the briefings Mr…'

'Kenneth.'

'Kenneth. The point is…'

'I know. I'm winding you up. I'm mental me.'

'Ha ha.'

'No I am, it's no joke love, I really am mental in the head, and I've got a psychiatrist and everything.'

'Oh, I'm so sorry, I thought you were joking.'

'It's no laughing matter, mental illness. You of all people should know that.'

'No, of course not… Funny, I don't remember seeing anything like that in your notes… You're doing it again aren't you?'

'Just having a laugh love, no harm done. Just getting through the day.'

'OK. Right. Ken.'

'Kenneth.'

'So: all men are mortal, Socrates…'

'Well first of all, all men haven't died yet have they? There's still some breathing. So you can't know if they're going to die or not, till they do. Can you? Not know for sure I mean. I mean, you can guess, but until every single one of them's died, how can you know? And the thing is, if you were still alive to know, then how would you know that you yourself was mortal? Cos if you were dead, then you wouldn't know anything would you? But if you weren't dead, then you'd be alive, so you couldn't know if you were mortal or not. Yet. Isn't that logic?'

'Mr. Medcrupp…'

'Second of all, how do you know some men aren't aliens who live forever but who look like people?' (Crafty look.) 'Eh? How would you know? You see, you can't know everything can you, not even you with your file. I could be one. Prove I'm not. Go on. You tell me.'

'No, Kenneth...'

'Ken.'

'... you have to say true or false. All men...'

'All men are aliens. I am an alien. Therefore I'm all men. Was that it?'

'No...'

'It's alright, I'm winding you up love. Don't take it so serious. I am an alien though. D'you want to see my antenna? Only pulling your leg.'

Aggregate score: 0.15

June Ireland, (46), DOB: 11/7/57

'Socrates? Socrates? You're having a laugh aren't you? And what about the ladies anyhow, don't they get a look in anywhere around here?'

'OK. All women are mortal, Socrates was, erm...'

'A woman?'

'No, OK, Helen. Helen was a woman...'

'What, Helen off Big Brother?'

'Actually I was thinking of Helen of Troy, but yes if you like...'

'Helen off Big Brother? She's mortal is she? I never saw that in the paper.'

'True or false?'

'If you say so love. I can't say I've ever really given the matter much attention to be honest with you. But if you're telling me Socrates was a woman, well then I suppose I've got to believe you haven't I? I mean, you from the Social and all.'

'So the statement is true?'

'If you say so.'

'No I'm not saying it's actually true…'

'So it's a lie.'

'Well no not really a lie, I only need to know if you think it's true or not.'

'So some of those things you've got in your book there are porkies? Shouldn't you be ashamed of yourself? You had me going there with Socrates and all for a minute.'

'No but you see that's the whole point…'

'You need me to tell you which ones are true.' June sits back grandly, narrowing her eyes, blowing her fragrant smoke over Mel's shoulder. 'It's always the way. Tell me this, June, tell me will he fall in love with me, tell me will I have a boy or a girl…'

'No, June, I'm not asking you to predict anything, I only want to know what you think.'

'I think a lot of things girlie.' Mysteriously affronted now, she shakes her head and stares out at the garden where a lanky, graceless girl, Kelly, is doing an angular version of gymnastic dancing. 'You don't know the half of it.'

Aggregate score: 0.08

Kelly Ireland, (14), DOB: 22/3/89

'OK, Kelly. Now I'm going to…'

'Ask me questions.'

'Yes, and you're going…'

'Yeah I know. OK, go.'

'Right. If all animals move, and no plants move, then anything that moves must be an animal.'

'Yeah?'

'No I'm asking you, true or false.'

(Giggles.) 'Dunno.'

'True or false Kelly? If all…'

'Dunno. True. False.' (Giggles, hides head in sweatshirt hood, twists hair around finger. Giggles. Mel sits up straighter. Smiles.)

'OK Kelly. If it takes you an hour to walk a mile, it'll take two hours to walk two miles.'

'You what? Dunno. Say it again.'

'If it takes…'

'True. Dunno.' (Giggles.) 'Dunno. Ten miles.' (Giggles.)

Aggregate score: 0.04.

May

8

Mel's first house visit to the Medcrupp/Ireland's was, in accordance with the Copenhagen Experiment protocols, a short one. It was arranged that she would be a guest at their evening meal, one windy May Thursday.

Having seen the whole tribe of them all at once at the meeting at the Mentorn Hotel, Mel was, she felt, ready to get up close and personal. Her three years at Family Welfare had taught her much about people; how to look, how to speak, how to listen. She chose her clothes with enormous care – not too formal, not too casual, and most of all nothing that could in any way be interpreted as threatening – and set off in good hopes.

Whitehawk has one advantage over most of the rest of Brighton: you can, at least, park. Mel pulled up beside the house and took a good long look at it. Seventies semi, small patch of green at the front and cracked cement path, a side passage suggesting the existence of a back garden. White-framed uPVC windows, white door and a small porch with blistered glass panes. Like most of the Whitehawk housing stock, the inhabited sections of it anyway, it was in good repair. Next door, she noted, was boarded up, the chipboard panels perfunctorily graffitied, a grill fitted over the door. Evidence of smoke damage from an upstairs window.

The right to buy had barely taken hold here, but you could see carriage lamps or big fancy window shutters here and there as evidence of ownership, and the occasional defiant For Sale sign, though buyers here would certainly be few. But still that sense of distance. A mere few hundred yards away to the south was showy Sussex Square, where a lower-ground-floor-back studio flat (without access to garden) now cost more than any one of these neat two and three bed semis or maisonettes. Roedean school was almost within spitting distance: it ought to be possible to hear the shouts from the lacrosse field. But Whitehawk is not Brighton.

Mel sternly corralled her thoughts back into shape, checked her hair and make-up once again, and with a deep sigh opened her door and stepped out into the warm air.

The front door was opened by a boy of about eight with another one standing close behind him, wrapped from head to toe in a floral duvet cover. The twins: what were their names?

'Hello sweetheart, I'm here to…'

'Mum!'

He disappeared down the passage yelling 'Mum!', the duvet-clad figure shuffling behind him. Mel stood at the door and felt the familiar reluctance to enter someone else's house, someone else's life. Within moments, she felt, she would be sucked in, the door would close, and she would be immersed in it all.

Nothing happened for a few seconds, Mel standing patiently as she waited to be admitted. Then a large grey blurry figure approached from the end of the hall. This time Mel had the name straight: June.

'June? Hi, I hope I'm not late…'

Half an hour in, and everything was going well. The family were eating in the kitchen/dining room/front room, which was all knocked through, seemingly expressly to allow the smaller of the children to race about and scream unhindered by any walls. Adults, meanwhile, were blessedly able to hear the activities of the children from any part of the house.

She took in the decor: snowy white carpets, new-bought furniture in green and gold with enormous padded sculptural excrescences, giant telly. On the creamy walls huge mahogany-framed oval studio portraits of children in school uniform, soft-focus, over-life-size and frighteningly colourful, and some rather similar pictures of dogs. Glass fronted cabinets, the glass shelves swarming with decorative porcelain – elegant ladies, tramps with violins, Laurel and Hardy, Princess Di, more dogs – plus large-format picture books on Monet, Constable, Degas, thick padded volumes that could have been photograph albums, racks of unmarked videos, and everywhere underfoot the many sharp and harshly-coloured plastic objects discarded by the frantic children.

Mel had done her homework, but was still having some difficulty putting faces to names. The population of the house was both large and very fluid, and the numbers of children rose and fell unaccountably. It's a maze in reverse, her supervisor had told her. Start at the centre and work outwards. June.

She sat at the bleached-elm-effect dining table, wedged in rather uncomfortably, with a weaselly adult to her right and a teenager to her left. The younger children were allowed to eat watching the television, but with the sound low. The colour, however, was on full, as if to compensate. Food was transferred to mouth without the eyes ever leaving the screen. They had glasses of viscous, orange liquid, unnaturally vivid, as if real life had the colour turned up as well.

June had delayed serving the adults until Mel arrived. The

food was much as she expected – chicken drummers, nuggets, oven chips, frozen veg. Everything was a uniform golden brown colour, except the token vegetable – courgette – which was beige. Nothing tasted of anything at all, except salt and fat and a faintly fishy smell from the chicken. Mel sat and smiled and behaved non-threateningly. There was no sign of Kenneth.

'So June. Looks like you've got your hands full on the catering front,' she said.

'Sorry love, I was miles away… Danny, don't… Lauren, don't let Danny… I said!… sorry love, you were saying…'

June's face, when she transferred her attention to Mel, was full of a warm, nurturing, quizzical quality that Mel quickly discovered meant nothing at all. The flesh in her face was grey. She was exhausted.

'I was saying, you've got your hands full…'

'Corinne! If I have to come over there… er, Corinne, sorry, what did I say?…'

Mel attempted to continue. 'With all the cooking.'

'Yeah well there's no one but me to see to it so…'

'That was smashing love,' said the adult to Mel's right, who had, amazingly, finished already, though the courgette clearly hadn't been much of a hit with him. 'Lovely bit of dinner that.'

'So June, are you going to introduce me round? I'm Mel,' she said, smiling as generally as she could and trying to meet as many eyes as were available: few were.

June reeled off some names, but Mel wasn't sure which person was indicated by which name, and didn't try to remember them. There would be plenty of time for names. Right now, she must be pleasant, submissive and as unobtrusive as possible.

'Oh I'll never get everybody straight,' she said, wishing to sound helplessly beguiled by them all. June gave Mel her Mother Courage face.

'It's all in your little file though isn't it? Who we all are?'

Mel couldn't pretend not to hear the intonation in 'little file'.

'Yes but that's probably all wrong,' Mel said, ingratiatingly, 'that's why I need to get to know you all in person a bit.'

'Why's the file wrong?' This was Kelly, a scrawny fourteen year old, June's daughter (Kenneth had come along later) though hardly favouring her. Tall, angular, and with a fixed quizzical expression which she might well have learned from her mother. She was made-up like a synchronised swimmer, lots of aquamarine eyeliner and American-tan blusher. She also favoured the hair-severely-scraped-back look. Her voice was high and wispy, her sentences formed seemingly under the pressure of extreme self-consciousness, and delivered with a slightly incredulous intonation, as if she could scarcely believe she was present at all, let alone speaking. She appeared very highly strung. She ate almost nothing, Mel noted, but merely cut and mashed her food, taking sly looks round the table as she did so.

'Well not wrong exactly, but really it only says date of birth and who's related to who and so on. It doesn't tell me what you're like. From the file, I'd never have known you were so pretty, Kelly,' she said.

Mel had never found it easy or natural to make comments of that kind, but she was suddenly feeling the need for it, for some straight-forward old-fashioned flattery. It was a big weapon, and it rarely failed. Kelly, obligingly, almost crumpled with gratification, and sent first June and then Mel a whole battery of bashful smiles in return. Mel saw June reach over and squeeze Kelly's cold bony hand.

'Not pretty...' Kelly said, wriggling in her seat and fiddling with a strand of hair. It was a love-in. The weaselly adult to Mel's right somewhat spoiled the moment by saying 'Does it say how pretty I am, your file?' and getting some sniggering from the other side of the table, but Mel ignored him. She was fairly certain he wasn't a permanent part of the Medcrupp/Ireland household and so she didn't really have to think about him. She had enough to do as it was. One at a time. June, Kelly, and who else…?

'So, no Kenneth then?' she enquired brightly of June, who cast her eyes in many directions, shook her head, bit her lip, blew hair up from her mouth into her face, fiddled with an ear, raised eyebrows. Aha, thought Mel, non-verbal communications expert, aha. Something there then.

'He comes and he goes, Kenneth…'

'Sometimes he comes.'

'And sometime he goes…'

'…and no-one knows where…'

'…and no-one knows why…'

This was some kind of familial comedy routine kicking in here, Mel thought, and managed a big friendly laugh. But where was Kenneth? The visit had been arranged, with some considerable difficulty, precisely so that all the members of the client family would be present. Everyone's convenience had been so exhaustively consulted that his absence could really only suggest that he was, as yet, not wholly on board as far as the project was concerned. Hearts and minds, as her supervisor had also told her; but hearts first.

'Also, I don't think I've seen… is it Dane…?' Mel said, matching June quizzical for quizzical. June was iron.

'You won't be seeing Dane,' June said, and Mel suddenly felt some grit under the surface. Kelly stared down at her plate and sniffed, to the accompaniment of annoyed glances from June.

'No, Dane's away at present.'

'Oh I see. He's what, nineteen now? Off on his travels I suppose?'

Another silence of the kind that this family was so expert in manufacturing descended, but Mel was, she thought, getting the hang of them a bit now, and risked persisting with her enquiring face to June. It was another adult, though, who answered her, a large blonde silent man on the other side of the table, the sniggering companion of the weaselly one, Mel noted.

'Yup. Off on his travels is Dane.'

'Have you got a picture of him? I'd love to see him.'

More silence. Kelly stood up suddenly and went out of the room, and June started collecting plates and looking busy.

'I was wondering if you wouldn't mind giving me a hand, in the kitchen,' June said, and no one within earshot could possibly mistake the tone. Mel followed June into the kitchen, which was spotless and staggeringly well-equipped. June started putting things into the dishwasher, then stopped and faced Mel. They were suddenly very close, and Mel was again struck by June's all-in-one purdah, her colourlessness, her exhausted vitality.

'Dane…' she said, and allowed her eyes to wander out to the back garden. 'Well Dane…'

'June, have I said something I shouldn't? It's only that Dane is in my file as resident here. I don't remember seeing him at the family conference. Is that wrong? That he lives here?'

'He did. Now he doesn't. Look, the thing about Dane… I mean he never paid me no rent or nothing…'

Mel stepped back immediately from the subject.

'Oh well, it won't make the slightest difference. I'll cross him off my list that's all…'

June was still struggling for some kind of explanation, but Mel cut her off.

'June. You're not to worry about anything. I'm not trying to interrogate you. If the file's wrong then I'll put it right. That's all there is to it.'

June sighed and made a small clicking sound. She was messing about with some kind of tea.

'Would you like a cup love? It's herbal.'

'Lovely, thanks June,' Mel said, and took the mug. The tea was very sweet, but with some kind of nagging bitter aftertaste that Mel couldn't place. She put the mug down again.

Suddenly Kelly was back in the kitchen, and urgently pushing something into Mel's hand: it was a photograph of a male, sixteen or seventeen she guessed. He was reclining on a slatted white vinyl lounger in brilliant sunlight, slick with sun cream, smoke curling from his fist. Mel needed about a thousandth of a second to see that he was a muscular capable-looking lad wearing swimming trunks and a come-and-get-it expression, like, she thought distantly, the 'street' one in a boy band. The shot was taken from the feet upwards, so much of the frame was taken up with spread-eagled thighs and well-stuffed Speedos. Dane had his hands folded behind his head, one knee was raised slightly. He had this ferocious smile... June took the picture away and handed it back to Kelly.

'Put it back love.'

'She said she wanted to see...'

'Put it back Kelly.' June kept her back to Mel, still staring out into the garden. There was a large cement shed at the far end with an unusually secure-looking door with a large, rusty padlock. More of an outbuilding than a shed. 'That was when he came to visit last year,' Kelly said, in her autumn leaves voice, and June's back stiffened. 'But he's not coming this year is he Mum?'

'Not this year Kelly.'

'Oh I hope he's alright,' Mel said, and June turned to face her.

'He's fine. He's in Cornwall. Working in a hotel...'

'Mum...'

'One minute, Madame. In a hotel. Commis chef.'

'Oh! Fantastic!' Mel said. 'And he's Mr. Medcrupp's nephew? That's right isn't it?' she said, pursing her eyebrows to suggest that the family were so intricate and fascinating that she could hardly begin to comprehend them.

'He's Kenneth's sister's oldest, yes. Her and David.'

'But he stays here sometimes? I can't imagine why he would be in my file, it's only supposed to be people who are actually resident…'

'Yes well like I said. He was. Now he isn't.'

'OK. I'll cross him off my little list.' Mel, to humour June from earlier on, said 'little list' in a voice of her own, a mock Censorious Tory Minister voice, but June gave her nothing back, and she smiled instead, remembering that office jokes would certainly have no currency here.

Kelly was back. She needed dropping off at dance, her lift hadn't shown up, and Kenneth was nowhere to be seen. June gazed helplessly at her.

'You know I can't Kelly.'

The weaselly adult appeared in the kitchen doorway and seemed about to offer, but was silenced by a look from June.

'No you're alright Paulie.' She sighed grimly. 'Well there's nothing for it. We'll have to organise a taxi.'

Mel didn't lose a second.

'Let me. Whereabouts is it Kelly?'

'No no, we couldn't possibly…'

'No bother at all June. Glad to help. Kelly?'

'Out Hangleton way.'

Miles away to the west. A good twenty minute drive.

'Great! That's on my way.'

Kelly made an enquiring face to June, who shrugged.

'Well if you're sure.'

'Definitely. We'll be off then. Kelly?'

Kelly had to scamper about a bit collecting glittery bobbles and assembling the contents of no fewer than three separate make-up bags. Mel made conversation with the twins in the front room while she was waiting. Only one of them would speak, the other hid his head under cushions and giggled in a manner that Mel could only characterise as coquettish. He was still under the duvet cover, so hiding his head made no real difference.

'My dad's got a sword that's at least five foot long,' the other one said, and Mel tried to look pleased to hear it.

'Really?'

'Yeah in fact actually I think it might be bigger than that even. I've only seen it once. I touched it once. But no one else can. Not anyone. Not ever.'

'Well! Wow!'

'I've got a brother, but he won't talk to you today. We look exactly the same.'

'It must be nice, having a brother.'

'I've got loads.'

'Of brothers?'

He nodded his head solemnly and stroked one forearm in a way that immediately called June to mind.

'In the shed.'

'Fantastic!'

'Actually, it's my dad's shed. It's massive.'

'It must be nice having a shed.' Mel was pretty much on automatic; eight year olds had never been her speciality, or boys for that matter. She was mostly listening out for Kelly to be ready.

'Actually my dad's got loads of sheds. He's got, about, twenty...'

'Gosh...'

'And they're all, like, massive?'

'Great! I can't wait to see them all. Well I think we're nearly off now...'

June arrived and was immediately deep in angry negotiation with the twins about baths, but managed a brave, brave smile for Mel as she said goodbye.

Kelly relaxed visibly in the car, even going as far as to light up. Mel wound the window down, but it had clearly not occurred to her passenger that Mel might prefer her not to smoke in the car. She exhaled out of the corner of her mouth, much in the June manner, and kept the cigarette held away from her body. Tiny ladylike drags, much nervy flicking of the ash. Her eyeshadow flashed, and there were traces of some glittery substance on her cheeks. Fluffy purple bobble, tasteful gold earrings, long shiny turquoise nails. Roomy white quilted Adidas parka with fur-lined hood.

Mel drove down Whitehawk Way and within three minutes was out and back in Brighton. Again the physical isolation of Whitehawk, its dispiriting existence only as a single giant traffic island, a no-place going to nowhere, struck her. There was only really this one way out, back, to the real world, the land of the living; Brighton. Only this one arterial connection. Mel had done some introductory anatomy many years ago and Whitehawk reminded her of a diagram of a human organ, connected but distinct, its connections only those that are essential to its purpose. Except that this organ didn't seem to have any purpose, except to be there.

Brighton: the white and cream-painted luxury mansion blocks of Sussex Square, the cliff face of Marine Gate; crumbling sash windows and corkscrew fire escapes disappearing into lush, shady, secret back gardens; the presence, above all, of estate agencies. Whitehawk had none of these. Whitehawk folded itself up behind her, swallowed into the contours of the valley, like a magic trick. It had ceased to be.

'So. Your mum's not a driver then Kelly?'

Kelly issued a slightly contemptuous sideways jet of smoke.

'Kenneth's going to teach me soon, then I can drive myself.'

Kelly had taken on a new tone suddenly, Mel thought. From anorexic shadow to teen glamour puss. It had happened the moment she'd left June's side.

'I hear you're a dancer?'

Another snort.

'That's what they tell me.' The voice was still wispy and listless but had now taken on a derisive edge. She was gazing out of the side window, but Mel was sure that she was actually watching her own reflection. Then she said, 'No, with my mum right, she won't go out anymore.'

Mel recalled June and her psychiatric history, a referral to an expert in phobias and compulsive behaviour.

'What do you mean Kelly?'

'Like, at all? Ever? If the house was literally burning down right, she wouldn't come out right, she'd rather get burned up.'

'I know your mum had some problems a few years ago, but somehow I thought...'

'Won't leave the house. Won't go near: front door, back door, any window. Will go into back yard, but only in daylight and only in company.'

'But she was at the Mentorn Hotel meeting.'

'Yeah, and you should have seen what we had to do to get her there. You should see her sometimes, she like stands in front of the window and says, can you not see the curtains moving? Can you not see it?' Mel recalled June's glacial calm, her drooping eyelids. She looked at Kelly with a new sense of her capability. There was iron under the surface.

'What about shopping?'

'Lidl deliver.'

'Do you know why she's so scared?'

'Yeah I do.'

Nothing more, except twisted lips and lots of smoke. Mel backed away.

'It must be awful to be scared like that,' she said neutrally, and Kelly shrugged.

'I've been scared loads of times.'

'What kinds of things scare you Kelly?'

Kelly shook her head. 'Ghosts.'

'Really? Do you believe in ghosts then?'

'What do you mean? Believe in them?'

'Well I mean have you ever seen one?'

Derisive snort. 'Have I ever seen any ghosts? Only like loads and loads of times.'

'That must be frightening.'

'It's not all different ones, it's the same one but different times.'

'And is that what's frightening June as well? A ghost?'

Kelly shrugged and ground her cigarette end out on the dash below the radio. She was, Mel noted, not particularly well car-trained. Change of subject coming.

'So do you make, like, a shed-load of money?'

Mel laughed. 'What me? You're kidding.'

Kelly raised eyebrows. 'No. I thought you must make a lot of money. You've got a nice car, your clothes are really nice...'

'Thank you.'

'So I thought you must make a bit.'

'You wouldn't believe me if I told you.'

'But you have got your own flat and everything?'

'Of course.'

'I'd love to have my own place right. If I had my own place right do you know what I'd do? I'd invite people round and I'd be like, have whatever you like, stay as long as you like, it wouldn't bother me at all. Not at all.'

'Have you got anyone particular in mind Kelly?' Mel said, attempting to coax out Kelly's former, bashful self, but that was long gone.

'Just whoever really,' she said, stretching and yawning at the same time. 'Just anyone. As long as I got on with them. It's up here. On the left. Over there.'

Kelly got out and organised her bags.

'Thanks.'

'Welcome. Maybe I could give you a lift another time? If Kenneth can't?'

'My mum says you're going to be around for ages.'

'Hope so.'

'OK. Well, see you.' Mel watched as Kelly joined three other girls with similar hair and age and posture, all going into the building. Kelly was clearly trying to imitate their grace, their bearing, but, Mel noted, she didn't have it. She was what she was, a bony, angular fourteen year old. It was very difficult to imagine her as a dancer.

Kelly turned, Mel waved goodbye, and Kelly's face lit up into the most beautiful, awkward, and unreserved of smiles as she waved back. Hearts and minds, Mel thought as she pulled away. Hearts and minds.

9

The Copenhagen Protocols indicated the importance of monitoring the client family at all hours of the day and night. Sleepovers were an essential component, yielding much valuable material. The remark, 'catch them off their guard' was never actually articulated, but that was clearly the intention. A family, even the most insular and closeted, could hardly maintain all of its secrets at all times, and it was important to observe them both rising and retiring, as well as anything that might happen to occur during the hours of darkness. Further, the simple fact of sleeping under the same roof as the client family would inevitably help to normalise the presence of the stranger. There were opportunities for unscheduled meetings in pyjamas and dressing gowns on the stairs or outside the bathroom, for instance. Whereas sharing a meal was a simple matter of hospitality, sleeping a night under the same roof was an act of trust, intimacy. A bond.

Mel had arranged to arrive at the house at nine thirty. At a previous meeting it had been agreed, with some difficulty, that Kelly would sleep in the twins' room, and Mel would take her room for these occasions, once Kelly had cleared out anything that was to be regarded as private. At the time Kelly had been inclined to think herself hard done by; but the face that welcomed Mel to the door was flushed with excitement.

'I've moved all of my stuff out, but I haven't cleared out the drawers or the wardrobe or anything.'

'Kelly, honestly, it's only for one night, I'm not going to need anything like wardrobe space…'

'Is that all you've got?' Kelly indicated Mel's overnight sports bag.

'All I need.'

'You travel light.'

'It's the only way,' Mel said, and Kelly nodded very seriously.

'If I'm like sleeping over somewhere, I only take just exactly the least possible amount of things I need.'

'And it is only one night.'

'Anyway, anything you haven't remembered, I've probably got it,' Kelly said, woman to woman, and Mel assented gravely. Kelly took the bag up the stairs.

Kelly's room, a tiny box at the back of the house, had clearly been decorated with a twelve year old girl in mind. It was neat and prim, in pastel shades and muted neutrals, with the use of plum and white gingham for the curtains and the decorative trimmings on the child-size dressing table. The walls carried evidence of the now older, more sophisticated Kelly: beefcake boybands and a poster of a dancer, barefoot, her feet immaculately pointed. There were a great many photographs, arranged in artful groups of three and six, of Kelly with various friends at her side, all posturing and grinning wildly in a variety of costumes and make-up effects: witches, cats, gangsters. Kelly's friends had a generic similarity, Mel thought, not only because of the facts of age and sex, but through a shared language of details, accessories and gesture: scraped back hair with a glittery clip, sparkly headbands, sequins under the eyes, aquamarine and jade and tangerine eye liner, as if they were unconsciously attempting a revival of Flashdance. All the girls she had known at school who were 'into dance' had been like this, she reflected. It was a very conservative world, closed to outsiders, a kind of anorectic freemasonry.

Kelly dropped Mel's bag onto the bed and, like a hotel porter angling for a tip, opened the window and turned down the cover. From next door came the low droning sound of one of the twins, who was seemingly chanting or reciting something. Mel shut the door.

'Now Kelly, I want to be absolutely certain that there is nothing in here you wouldn't want me to know about. Obviously I'm not going to be poking around in your things, but if there's anything at all…'

'No that's OK,' she said emphatically, 'I've got it all safe.'

Mel's eye fell onto a photograph which was stuck to the wall by the bed, all by itself: Dane grinning his hormonally supercharged smile, with Kelly in front of him. They were on the deck of a ship. Dane's hand was resting on Kelly's shoulder, and her hair was blowing all over her face. Kelly followed Mel's eye.

'That's me and my cousin Dane,' she explained formally, standing slightly more stiffly as she spoke. 'We get on, like, really well.'

'So I see,' Mel said.

Back downstairs, June and Kenneth were winding down from the day in front of a wildlife programme. June, Mel noted, was having some of her herbal remedy, the smell of which was resonating all over the ground floor. They both craned their heads to welcome her as she came in, and June indicated where she should sit. The immense television – needle-sharp picture, screamingly vivid colour and terrifyingly powerful sound, though kept low for the time being – showed an Antarctic wasteland, frozen sacks of blubber mewling in desperate seas full of shattered ice.

'Got everything you need up there love?' June enquired, and Mel said she had. The weaselly adult – Paulie? – emerged from the kitchen and took a chair next to Kenneth.

'You know what this reminds me of Kenneth?' June said. 'When Kelly used to have all her mates over. Remember? They all used to sleep on the floor down here. Practising steps and that? Remember Kenneth?'

Kenneth, unable, seemingly, to sit still for more than a few seconds at a time, was back on his feet, on his toes even, arms spread wide, and head thrown back.

'Like this?'

He took a few steps and attempted a twirl, while Paulie smirked and June shook her head: mental! But Mel couldn't help noticing that Kenneth had all the natural grace that Kelly so obviously lacked; even in parody he was supple and expressive, and that was allowing for blubber belly and stumpy legs.

'Well it's obvious where Kelly gets her talent from,' Mel said, half a second before she remembered that Kelly was not, in fact, Kenneth's daughter. Silence, followed by a nasty sound from weaselly man. Mel found herself starting to dislike him. Thumping from upstairs.

'Kenneth, go and have a look at the twins would you love, I can still hear them,' June said, and Kenneth executed a mock salute.

'Do you want to come and say goodnight?' he said, turning to Mel. 'They've been talking about you all day.'

'Of course,' Mel said, surprised at the invitation, and followed Kenneth's heavy tread up to the twins' room.

There was scuffling as Kenneth opened the door, quick footsteps, and the sound of objects being dragged around.

'It's Smelly! Quick!' one of them screamed, and then a quivering silence.

'Aye aye you two. Now get to bed,' Kenneth said into the room. All Mel could see were two humps on bunk beds, and an inflatable mattress on the floor. 'And when Kelly does come in, if I hear one peep out of either of you…'

The humps were motionless.

'You're on parole now. The both of you. What does that mean? Michael, what does that mean, what I said to you?'

One hump produced a face, gleaming in the dark.

'Means you'll get all arsey about it later.' The other hump started shaking at 'arsey'.

'No, genius, it means I'm trusting you. You're on your word. If I hear one complaint from Kelly tomorrow, I'm warning you you'll be on the right road to smacked legs…'

Both humps were quivering again now.

'If you upset her, then I'm going to come and upset you. Got it? The pair of yous? Now say goodnight to Mel. She's come up special.'

One head emerged again, the same as before.

'Goodnight Meeeel,' he said in a drawling voice. 'Sleep tiiiight don't let the bedbugs biiiite.'

'Goodnight Michael. Goodnight David,' she said, and immediately the other hump was in paroxysms. Kenneth went over and kissed them both goodnight. 'See you tomorrow guys.'

'I feel terrible causing all this chaos,' Mel said as they went down again.

'Oh they love it. Bit of excitement.'

'Kelly will be alright won't she? I feel like I'm turfing her out of her own room…'

'No she's brilliant with them, Kelly. She loves children,' he said, firmly.

Back downstairs June's smoke had clearly begun to take effect: she was slumped further back on the couch, her eyes barely focused on the giant telly where a particularly appealing penguin, barely fledged, was meeting a seal with a keen sense of fun. Slo-mo of the spray of blood as the penguin was merrily ripped in two. June looked on approvingly. "And so we see…"

June absently offered the joint to Mel, who politely refused. Paulie reached for it instead. 'Over here love.'

June was soon ready for bed, a fact she signified by locking the back door. Mel noticed that she did this several times, rattling the handle each time.

'OK, I'm going up love.'

'I'll be up in a minute love.'

June made her slightly woozy way upstairs, and Kenneth and Paulie rearranged themselves more luxuriously in front of the telly. Penguins huddled in some nightmare of blizzard and darkness and predation. Paulie was soon nodding off, and Mel was about to turn in herself when June reappeared, still in the grey sweats, her hair loose now.

'I thought I'd better show you about the immersion,' she said, and Mel followed her up to the bathroom.

'Actually it wasn't about that at all,' June said, locking the door behind them and coming closer to Mel than she cared for. The bathroom was intimidatingly brightly lit. Towels in co-ordinating pastel shades on heated chrome rails, and an extraordinary array of grooming products. Mel sat on the edge of the bath. June was wild and somewhat unfocused, chaotic hair, bleary eyes, dry lips.

'Oh?'

'I thought someone should say.'

'Say…?'

'At night. Oh love I don't know where to start. Things…' June's voice had dropped to a whisper. Her eyes scanned Mel's face restlessly. Her cigarette smoke began to fill the room almost immediately.

'Things…?'

'…happen. At night.'

'I see.'

'I doubt it love. We get… there are…'

'I'm listening June.'

'We get visitors.'

'June, I'm not sure I'm understanding you here…'

'I can protect you. To some extent.'

'Protect me?'

'I thought you should know. If you're going to be under our roof overnight. Kenneth said not to mention anything, but I thought it was only fair that you should know.'

'June…'

June put her fingers against Mel's lips, in a shushing gesture which Mel, frankly, found rather annoying.

'Can't say anymore for now. Everything will be fine. And if…'

'If…?'

'If you should hear anything, you remember. Nothing here will hurt you.'

'June, I'm none the wiser really.'

The door handle was shaken from the other side.

'Minute!' June called out, and shushed Mel again. Mel was unpleasantly struck by how cold and clammy June's hands were. 'We'll say no more for now,' she said, and pressed Mel's wrist with a surprisingly powerful grip. 'Everything's going to be fine,' she whispered again, dropped her cigarette end into the pan, and flushed the toilet.

On the landing Mel met Kelly, clutching a batch of papers of some kind, which she was in the process of removing from her room. The twins' door was open, and Mel could hear Kenneth messing about with something in there.

'He's putting me up a screen. Out of sheets.'

'That's thoughtful.'

'It's only for one night.'

'OK. Well I think I'll probably turn in,' Mel said, suddenly desperate to be away from them all so she could think. 'As long as you're sure you've got everything…'

'Yeah. I forgot about these…' Kelly said, holding the papers closer. Mel could see that they were closely hand-written, in many coloured inks, with a lot of exclamation marks and glittery stars. 'Goodnight then Mel.'

'Goodnight Kelly.' As she shut Kelly's door she heard Kenneth issuing further, more comprehensive, threats to the twins about good behaviour and the consequences of upsetting Kelly. Mel was pleased to see a small brass-coloured bolt on the door, and pushed it to. The room was neat and clean, almost impersonal, except for Kelly's pictures. She could hear the drone of the television from below, and music from somewhere else, somewhere nearby. Opera, a soprano voice, climbing and climbing, straining up towards some unimaginable peak of longing. Mel sat and then lay on the bed, closed her eyes, allowed her sense of herself to return, gradually, as the noises and the music subsided around her. It was a warm still night. She even thought she could hear the waves breaking on the shingle from far away. She thought, I should write up my notes…

Screaming!
What time is it?
The room was dark and hot, there was screaming coming from somewhere. Mel fought off the feeling of unreality and forced herself properly awake. She groped her way to the door, fumbled for the light switch, failed to find it. She tried to open the door. Wouldn't open. Screaming, heavy footfalls, several voices, and another sound, a sound which was strangely familiar, as if she had recently been dreaming about it. Was it singing? She tried to shake off the blurriness in her head, but all she could think of was what time is it, why won't the door open?

She wrenched the handle this way and that, shook it, even tried a few kicks. It was completely solid.
'June? Kenneth?'
The screaming was from nearby, inside the house, and was now counterpointed by other voices. Rapid thumping up and down the stairs, shouts.

'Hello? Anybody?' The room was nightmarishly hot. She felt a bubble of panic rising up and swallowed it down. 'June? Could somebody open the door please?'

No response. The voices were coming from downstairs now. Kelly's voice, high, shaky, hysterical. June's voice attempting reassurance. Some baritone grunts from Kenneth. Mel heard isolated fragments: I heard him! – Kelly will you be still for one minute – He's outside, I heard him!

Mel shook the bedroom door violently.
'Hello? I can't get out! Hello!' There was no answer. Mel stood staring stupidly at the door. Then there was a polite tapping

from the other side. Mel froze with inexplicable terror.

'Hello?'

She heard another knock, then a familiar giggle: one of the twins. Relief flooded her body. The backs of her knees were dripping.

'Michael? David? I can't get the door open. Do you think you could get your dad a minute…?'

'My name's not Michael.'

'My name's not David.'

'OK. Look, whoever it is. Can you open the door?' More giggling. Footsteps retreating. Dammit, there must be a light switch somewhere. She heard voices from the garden. She opened the window and a great gust of cool air splashed her. She could see a lurking figure in the gloom of the garden, down by the shed.

'Hello?'

The figure turned, hunched and malign, and again she felt a slow shock of fear.

'Kenneth? Is it? Can you hear me?' She was oddly inhibited from shouting out into this suburban-seeming back garden in the middle of the night, but she could feel her patience running out by the second.

No response. This, she thought, was getting ridiculous.

'Look, I seem to be locked in,' she spoke, not loud but very clearly into the darkness. 'Hello? Could someone come and let me out please?'

Nothing. The eeriness of gardens in the dark. The shadowy figure melted away, not unlike – she thought unwillingly – a ghost.

The door rattled in its frame behind her.

'Love? It's on your side.' Kenneth's voice.

'What? Kenneth, I can't get…'

'The bolt. It's on your side. You must have locked it.'

The action was all coming from the kitchen. As Mel entered, brushing her hair back from her face, she saw Kelly being restrained by June in a kind of desperate bear hug. Kelly was still screaming, her face contorted, her whole body rigid and clonic, as June tried to soothe.

'June?' Mel spoke in a carefully modulated tone, low and gentle but very competent. 'June, is there anything I can do to help?'

June turned a frantic face to her, shook her head and crazy hair.

Kelly's screams were moderating now, giving way to some extremely unattractive snorting and gulping noises. She was still being held tight by June. Mel caught some movement from the darkened garden in the window and immediately Kelly was arcing and screaming again.

'He's out there!'

Mel pushed past the two and wrenched the back door open, to June's evident horror: she shrank back from the doorway, pulling Kelly with her. Mel peered out into the garden.

'Hello? Is there someone out here? Hello?'

The garden was long and narrow, with the shed at the far end half overgrown with buddleia and brambles, and not much else except a rusty old barbecue and partially burnt plastic toys. Two steps led down from the kitchen door, then a brick patio arrangement, then patchy grass. Light from the kitchen spilled out onto the patio, but after that all was gloom and shadow. Mel took a few steps.

'Hello?'

Mel felt Kenneth at her shoulder, and breathed in his ear: 'Can you see anything?'

'Let's have a look love.'

Kenneth went ahead into the garden. Mel noted, with some

surprise, that he gestured as he went, a sort of scything, sweeping motion, accompanied by guttural sounds which could have been 'git' or 'get'.

Then Kenneth stiffened – Kelly and June became still and silent – Kenneth abruptly lunged, almost fell, he was thrashing in the mud. A single, powerful shriek from Kelly. Kenneth was grunting, he was wrestling with something Mel couldn't see, she tried to come forward to help him but her legs were oddly incapacitated, her head still full of a thick buzzing distance from the scene. Kenneth was back on his feet, he was kicking out wildly, lost his footing again, was back down in the mud.

'Git. G'waaaaan!'

Kenneth struggled upright again, he was chasing back and forth across the bottom of the garden, by the shed, then he was gesturing and yelling at the back wall.

'Git now! I'm warning you…'

He stopped. No-one moved. He turned and faced Mel and the two in the kitchen. Shrugged.

'Well. He's gone again. For now…'

Kenneth, mud-caked like a rugby player, walked back up the garden, past Mel, and slowly into the kitchen, where Kelly was now composedly sobbing, and June was starting to look like she wanted more herbal remedy.

Mel stood a few moments in the garden. From an open upstairs window she could hear the twins, an antiphonal call and response: 'My name is not Michael, David!' – 'My name is not David, Michael!', repeated endlessly back and forth. She could see shadows from their bedroom, two figures bouncing up and down uproariously before a sudden silence as Kenneth came into the room to tell them to pipe down, the flap was all over, and they were going the right way for a smacked bottom. Again Mel thought she heard something else, a faint trace of sound in the damp cool air, a vibration, strings, an oboe, tentatively, almost painfully, rising, an orchestra... it faded again. Mel came back inside. The sofa, she noted absently, was made up into a bed with a big floral duvet and two pillows, showing signs of recent occupancy. She shut it all out of her mind and went back to her room. This time she didn't lock the door. She opened her laptop and stared at the screen for a few blank minutes. Log entry, Tuesday 15th...

Jesus, she thought. I mean, Jesus. Where do you start?

10

Mel was struggling to find the right words, the right register. She chewed her lower lip as she tapped away.

Profiles/overviews.

'June Ireland.'

'June is 48 years old. She and Kenneth have been partners for more than fourteen years. There are three children, Kelly, fourteen (from a previous relationship of June's), and the twins Michael and David, eight.'

'June, who was born on the Whitehawk estate, left school at fifteen and went to work in a nearby launderette. Her relationship with Kelly's father, Gary Chope, ended when Kelly was born. June and Kenneth met through Kenneth's business activities.'

'For the last fifteen years, June has been in receipt of Disability Living Allowance. She has been unable to work because of a cluster of psychological impairments which includes agoraphobia, acute anxiety states, insomnia and depression. The onset of this condition is roughly contemporaneous with her first meeting with Kenneth Medcrupp, and also coincides with her pregnancy with Kelly. Within the last twelve months June has developed a morbid terror of the back garden, the front garden, and the side passage of the house. She is terrified of the area around the front door, the back door, and refuses to stand close to the windows. Attempts to address this problem through, first counselling, and then a short period of psychotherapy, have proved to be of no value. She presents her agoraphobia as a fear of the supernatural, specifically of a ghost (cf Kelly Ireland below). June has been prescribed the anti-depressant Cipramil, which leaves her feeling 'woolly'.'

Mel paused. The next sentence was tricky.

'June is also an adherent of a herbal remedy, which she self-prescribes and self-administers.'

Hm.

'This medication also makes her feel 'woolly'. It is administered throughout the day as needed.'

Jamie raised his eyebrows. He was reading from behind her shoulder, a habit which she was fully intending to get him out of.

'So,' he said, 'if I may paraphrase? She's got three kids, no job, she's on permanent sick for some made-up condition, and she sits around on her fat arse in a council house all day smoking dope and seeing ghosts. Correct?'

'No-one likes a smart-arse, Jamie.' She doggedly typed on.

'Kelly Ireland.'

'Kelly, 14, is June's oldest child. Kelly has a history of truancy from school, petty theft, and has been cautioned by the police on three occasions for disorderly behaviour, including attempted damage to a post box when she was eleven.'

'Kelly has within the last twelve months stopped attending

76

school at all, preferring to 'help' June at home. Kelly has been referred by her GP (Dr French) to an eating disorders specialist, who has diagnosed her as borderline anorexic, with an anxiety condition around the subject of food. Her weight has been low but stable for several months. Part of Kelly's condition is an addiction to exercise, in her case 'dance'. She attends classes three times per week, and has extra coaching sessions in addition to that. Dance is a major preoccupation, not only for Kelly, but for everyone in the household.'

'Kelly, while not suffering from her mother's agoraphobia, has also seen the ghost...'

'Mel...'

'I know what you're going to say Jamie...'

'"Kelly is a fucked-up dipstick like her barking mother..."'

'Easy for you to say. We, at Social Services, must say it differently. And for my next trick...'

'Kenneth Medcrupp.'

Kenneth is 48 years old, and has lived on Whitehawk all of his life, with the exceptions of his time in the navy and a short period of remand nine years ago.

Kenneth's work status is a vexed issue. He describes himself as a self-employed business man, but his records indicate that he has been in receipt of various benefits for most of the last twenty years. An investigation into his affairs conducted by the Inland Revenue five years ago resulted in an attempt to prosecute him for tax evasion, though Kenneth maintains that his activities were purely philanthropic and generated no income. Kenneth is in receipt of Carer's Attendance Allowance for June, and also receives a Mobility Allowance himself for a condition which has been diagnosed as...'

'Don't tell me. It couldn't be a bad back could it?'

'… a serious and debilitating recurring lumbar problem…'

'Golden backache. I thought you had to be in the police to get that.'

'Yes well Kenneth's found a loophole hasn't he.'

'Lifetime on the sick. No mortgage, no commuting and no income tax. Sounds fairly rational to me. Sounds like he's been "Thinking it Through" to me,' Jamie said. Mel ignored him. Where to start with the twins, she was thinking? She sat back and considered.

She'd found them in the back garden: at first she'd thought they were dancing. As ever, one of them was completely covered in the duvet cover. She had resigned herself to never knowing for sure which was which, was already fairly certain they never gave their true names anyway, and was starting to harbour the demoralising suspicion that it wasn't always the same one covered up.

They were standing a few feet apart. The covered one was completely still, while the other executed what she thought might be some kind of martial arts technique, knees histrionically bent, arms outstretched. But as she got closer she realised with a flash of dismay that he was in fact armed with some kind of knife, a big one, with which he was slashing the air a horrific few millimetres away from the shrouded head.

'Michael?'

She ran the last few steps and grabbed his arm, jerked him round to face her.

'For God's sake! What do you think you're playing at?'

He regarded her calmly as she wrested the weapon from his hot fist. The blade was rusty, dark and ridged menacingly along its back, the handle warm and faintly sticky like old packing tape. Discoloured in parts. Jagged and pitted along the edge. Lethal. She was amazed to be holding such a thing. And there was some kind of engraving, words etched into the blade near the handle: she started to unwrap some of the leather binding to get a better look.

'Where did you get this?'

No answer. His gaze travelled behind her shoulder; she turned to see Kenneth bearing down on her, stripped to the waist in baggy pink shorts. He was moving faster than she could ever remember seeing him do before. His breasts and belly were rippling in a way that Mel was disturbed to find fascinating. She had a sudden and entirely unwelcome vision of him and June together, the flaps and the folds, the grunting, the sheer pouchy weight of it all. He reached her, panting.

'Don't you touch that! Don't you ever touch that! You throw that down right now. You hear me missy?'

He was hot and pulsing with rage. She stood, rooted with amazement and a slow flush of anger of her own. He was making her feel 12 years old. Had he been watching her? How had he suddenly appeared like this?

'Well, Kenneth,' she said, as coolly as her thumping heart and trembling voice would allow, 'I thought I should take it away from Michael…'

'My name is not Michael…'

'…before he took David's head off!' She laid it on the grass between them with elaborate care.

'I'll thank you to mind your business,' Kenneth said, quiet and cold now, a vein throbbing and ticking ominously on his fat neck. Breath and teeth and threat. 'I'll remind you you're a guest here. And this…' He indicated the sword '… this you don't touch, Capeech? Michael, bring it back inside. Right now mister.' He marched back into the house, his massive hams slamming the air aside. The garden shook with him.

Mel, furious, stood and met Michael's nerveless eye. She heard giggling from beneath the duvet cover. Michael picked up the blade and sauntered after Kenneth, swinging it insolently. The duvet ghost waddled importantly after him...

Michael and David Medcrupp.

Mel pondered for a while then decided to leave her report on the twins for another time. She was feeling in need of a drink.

11

Jamie had been badgered into listening to Mel's first report. Within seconds he was hiding his head under a cushion and moaning.

'Make it stop...'

'Jamie. It's not that bad.'

'It's terrible. It doesn't sound like English at all. It sounds, actually,' he said, his face reappearing briefly from its hiding place, 'as if it's been translated from Danish.'

'It's supposed to sound like that,' Mel said. 'It's supposed to sound scientific. I continue:

'"Initial evaluations using the Torrance/Barclay Protocol and Boyce Standardised Questionnaire have produced aggregate scores of as low as four percent in the case of Kelly Ireland. Critical and logical reasoning are hardly in evidence, and success in true/false determining (Kui/Varney) hardly better than chance. In place of these there is a set of belief matrices which..."'

'Hold on. Mel. "Belief matrices"?'

'What's wrong with that?'

'Why not say "beliefs"?'

'Because we're supposed to say belief matrices. Alright with you?'

'Fine by me. Is there very much of this?' Mel showed him her report. He made a happy face. 'Great.' He sighed and put his head back under the cushion. 'OK. Ready.'

'So anyway in place of these we have these belief matrices, OK? "Two adults and one child have been interviewed, and have reported systems of belief which demonstrate marked irrational and magical properties."'

'Really?'

'God yes. Honestly, you should see them, Jamie. They're completely deranged as far as I can tell.'

'So why not say that?'

'I continue: "...the extents of which have yet to be established fully. Preliminary appraisals however are indicative of..."'

'Mel, I'm sorry, this all sounds like absolute bollocks.'

'"...poorly-structured evaluative and analytical methodologies..."'

'Enough.'

She spoke louder. '"...partial or faulty cognitional resources..."'

'No such word. Cognitional.'

'Yeah there is. Like 'volitional'.'

'Yes, except that 'volitional' is a real word, whereas 'cognitional'...'

'Don't care. Sounds scientific. "...and a casual or wholly absent approach to reality-testing. Propositional reasoning, mathematical reasoning..."'

'Mel I'm going to kill you now. It's for the best. Generations to come will thank me.'

'Nearly there. "...and systemic heuristic sub-routines in the client group are all poorly developed." There. That wasn't so bad was it?'

Jamie gurgled from beneath the cushion. 'Yes it was.'

'Well I can assure you that my supervisor is going to fucking love it.'

12

'"… and systemic heuristic sub-routines are…"'

'Yes. Mel. I wonder if I could stop you there for a moment…' Richard, the supervisor, stroked his goatee and appeared thoughtful, possibly even soulful, Mel thought absently watching him. The room was tiny, in shades of buttermilk and cream, with louvered blinds and an enormous filing cabinet. Mel was uncomfortably hot, and Richard was far too close. Not helping matters at all was an electrically-operated object in white plastic, the purpose of which was to heat up small quantities of scented oil, in this case spicy orange, thus making the room stink and adding an indefinable but coercive air of mood management to proceedings. Richard was, Mel had been informed, a grand master of mood management, a virtuoso. He had whole vocabularies of raised eyebrows, mouth twitches, strokes of the side of the ear, crinkly smiles, every one of which was calibrated to some precise shade of emotional tone, all somehow amplified and made monstrous by the scented fumes. What did you call the thing anyway? An infuser? Mel hunted for the right word and couldn't find it. A crucible?

'Yes,' Richard was saying. 'Now in the OMP manual…'

She dragged her attention back to him. He was surprisingly

difficult to focus on, possibly because he was so extremely reflective. 'Sorry, the…?'

'Objectives, Methodologies and Protocols…'

'The big white ones.'

'Yes.' Pause, crinkle. 'That's right. The big white ring binders Mel. Anyway, in there you'll find a description of the kind of log we're looking for from our field operatives. There is, of course, a rigorous and highly structured, er, structure to the project, and, of course, findings will ultimately be expressed in the form of a formal paper, using all the appropriate language and so on. Your case studies will ultimately be written up in that form. But in the first instance, that isn't really what we're looking for.'

'It isn't?'

'Not really. For the evaluation phase what we want is much more like a diary, a journal. We want to hear your impressions – what you see, what you hear – rather than any attempt at a formal or clinical assessment. We want you to be our eyes and ears.'

'Bugger.'

'Not to worry. Early days.' Richard shrugged his lip and leaned forward, as if intending to pat her on the leg, then thought better of it and leaned even further back. 'I mean, for instance, what does the place look like?'

'What Whitehawk? You know what it looks like.'

'Yes. Of course. But for the purposes of your report it would be helpful if you were to describe it, briefly, so that your reader has a context. Is it a welcoming place, an intimidating place? Did you, for instance feel, at any time that your safety was at risk?'

'No…'

'Did anything about the appearance of the streets or the houses or the people strike you?'

'Apart from the extraordinary similarity to Versailles, you mean? Richard, they don't call it Shitehawk for nothing.'

'Yes, now I fear that we may have moved a shade too far in the opposite direction. Language-wise, I mean. Look, why not read up some of the original Danish reports – there's an appendix at the back of OMP with some examples – and then have another run at it? I'm not in any way suggesting that your findings are inaccurate, I'm suggesting that you might word them differently.'

'Bugger.'

'It's purely a matter of getting the tone right.'

'Can I say mad as a box of frogs?'

'I'd prefer it if you didn't. So I'll see you in a week's time and we'll talk again. Any problems, don't hesitate to…' he indicated the extent of his availability, his emotional generosity, the benignity of his aromas. Mel tried to look suitably grateful.

13

Mel caught her first glimpse of the wedding dress by accident, when she bumped into June on the landing the next Thursday. June could barely see over the immense heap of white, ivory and buttermilk fabric and pretty much walked straight into her, giving a shriek of surprise and dropping the whole thing.

'Christ! You gave me a fright there love.'

It was an enormous dress, involving not only a very full skirt and hugely flared sleeves, but also a train. But what caught Mel's eye most immediately was the fact that the dress, and the train, were decorated with three narrow black felt stripes, all the way down. Adidas stripes.

'June! Oh it's… wonderful! Can I see?' Mel said, and June, with some obvious reluctance, gathered the thing up and held it in front of her body, smoothing out the billows with the flat of her knuckly hand. Her hair stuck out madly from the top.

'Wow!'

Mel could, in truth, think of nothing to say; it was one of the most appalling objects she had recently seen. The material was shiny and synthetic with bits of lace and artificial pearls stuck all over it. The stripes were of black felt, hemmed and stitched with enormous, painful care to keep the lines straight. It was hideous.

'June!' Say something. 'It's sensational.'

'Not quite finished yet. I need to do some more beading on the bodice, and there a few darts at the waist that still aren't sitting quite right yet...'

'June! You made it? Yourself?'

'Of course.' Purring. 'Always was handy with a sewing machine. I make most of Kelly's outfits. As well, I mean, I make outfits for Kelly as well.'

'June, this is... Who's the lucky girl then?'

'Oh a friend actually, a friend of mine. Of Kelly's I mean.'

'This is such a beautiful job,' Mel said, gently fingering a seam. It really was an achievement, if taken solely on a technical level. 'Is it soon? The wedding?'

'Oh no. It's not for a while yet. But, you know, you can't leave everything to the last minute with a wedding.'

'I should say not. June, if I ever get hitched I want you to make the dress. OK?'

'Of course love. I'd be happy to. Can't see you in anything quite like this though.'

'Well. Maybe something a bit like that. I don't know if I'd really need the train...'

'I'm doing the bridesmaids' dresses as well, obviously. Peach and ivory. Slashed puffball sleeves, and then at the back it gathers into a bow, like BoPeep? Really lovely.'

'Quite a job.'

'It is love, yes. It's a lot of worry actually.'

'I bet.'

'They're 12, eight and five. And you know 12 year olds, they're growing every ten minutes...'

'Yes.'

'It is a worry. You know, so many things that can go wrong on the day...'

87

'Will you be there?'

'Will I...?'

'At the wedding? To see your creations?' June, Mel felt, was avoiding her eye; she held the dress like a shield. Defiant, but about what?

'Oh of course.' June looked away, looked back. See, Mel thought? Evasive too.

Later that day, Mel found herself at the landing window watching Kelly and her friend practising in the back garden. It was a long and complicated routine, and there were many stops and starts and a lot of dissension. Kelly and the friend were both dressed in tight cropped jeans (Kelly's with glittery hearts appliquéd), and very brief halter tops, (Kelly's with the remark 'SLUT' on the front). Kelly also wore a choker of black velvet. The routine involved them interlocking arms behind their backs and executing fast turns that made them both fall over in hysterics every time they tried it.

At some point Mel realised that she was not the only observer of this. A gesture from Kelly alerted her to the fact that someone else was watching, from the kitchen window. And a face Kelly pulled, a twisted upper lip and a downward duck of the head, told Mel who it was: Kenneth. The quality of the performance, Mel noted, went somewhat downhill from that point. Stiffer, more self-conscious, more laboured over. Not that it had really 'flowed' up to now. Mel remembered her own dancing days, thick-ankled, eight, wearing the wrong shoes, moist-eyed with jealousy and resentment of the other girls.

The back garden was baked dry, a pitilessly glaring enclosure, the grass scorched to straw, the soil not much more than dust, stunted shrubs gasping at the margins. The two girls were streaked and glistening with sweat, grass stalks adhering to them, flushed, panting. Tight muscular bellies, Mel noted.

Mel came down to the kitchen and saw Kenneth sitting in the open back door, feet up on the edge of the draining board, beer can in hand. Again bare-chested. Kenneth clearly had no shyness about his shape. The incident with the sword was seemingly forgotten about, he was in a sunlit pool of afternoon-off geniality.

'Hey! Come to watch the show?'

Mel pulled up a chair and joined him. The apology was taken for granted. 'What's her name? The friend?'

'Couldn't tell you love. She's never said. Too shy.'

The girls conferred tersely, like doubles tennis players on a losing streak, and separated. They struck poses, and then, presumably on a signal that Mel couldn't see, they ran towards each other. The intention, Mel thought, was that one of them would catch the other and swing her round, but what actually happened was a badly mistimed jump and the banging together of heads in a manner which – Mel felt certain – was not intended.

'Ouffff!' This was Kenneth's helpful response, delivered in an American sports announcer voice. 'That's gotta hurt.'

The routine continued, teetering on the edge of self-parody at every step. Mel found her attention wandering.

'So Kenneth. I hear there's a wedding coming up?'

No response. Then casually:

'Is that right?'

Mel sensed it instantly of course, the secret nature of the wedding, the betrayal of the secret by June, Mel's own complicity now in whatever the secret was. For the first time she understood the meaning of 'behind enemy lines'. She thought of the big thick white ring binders, Objectives/ Methodologies/ Protocols, all still wedged under the passenger seat. She waited a moment for the training to kick in.

Then she thought she'd probably have to manage without it.

'Yes, I ran into June with the dress. A friend of Kelly's I think June said?'

Nothing clear, but the relaxation of a foot that had been swinging fast, and a shift in a crease over an eyebrow. A long thirsty swig of beer. Nothing you could give a name to. Kenneth was giving nothing away. You would need computers to fathom Kenneth at this point.

'No good asking me love,' he said, and she was dismissed.

The routine stopped while Kelly squinted furiously up at an upstairs window. Then, a sulky teenage whine:

'Kenneth! Make them stop...'

Kenneth, sighing, stood and came out into the blinding garden, and yelled up at the back of the house.

'You two! If I have to come up there...'

He came back again to the kitchen.

'Michael and David,' he said, shifting his bulk back into the spindly chair. 'They do her. Well one of them does.' Kenneth did a quick parody of the twins' parody of Kelly's near-parodic dance, and Mel tried not to laugh, as did Kenneth.

'No really, it's not on,' he said with a serious face, in a loud voice, but with an 'artistic' flick of the hand and wrist, out of sight of Kelly. 'They've no right taking the piss like that. It's completely out of order.'

'Kenneth,' Mel said, without quite knowing how she was going to continue, 'the other night...'

'Hm?'

'I mean, when Kelly was upset, and we came out here, you and me...'

'Yes?' He was only half interested.

'Well. I suppose all I mean really is, what did Kelly see? What did you see? Because me, I didn't really – of course it was dark and everything, but I didn't actually see anything…' (except for the shadow slinking away behind the shed and the bins, that is, she thought, except for that).

'Wrong question.'

She looked straight at him, but got only the side of his face, his unreadable ear and jaw, a pendulous hairy tit in profile. 'What do you mean Kenneth?'

'Kelly didn't see anything.'

'She didn't?'

He shook his head slowly, still gazing directly out into the heat and scorch of the back garden.

'No. She heard something.'

'What did she hear?'

'Same thing she always hears.'

'Which is?'

'Ouffff!' He said again, as Kelly and the unnameable friend again collided, with a kind of tragic inevitability. He gave Mel a ribald poke in the ribs with an elbow.

'Kenneth? What did she hear? Did you hear it as well?'

'Howling.'

'Sorry?'

He paused and, with some obvious reluctance, gave her his complete attention for a moment. His whole face. The bristly lips, the redness of the tongue.

'Howling. She hears howling.'

'What kind… I mean who…?' Mel was absolutely at a loss. She'd thought she'd heard something, but it certainly wasn't that. She thought she'd heard singing.

'Not "who".'

Oh for Christ's sake Kenneth!, she yelled internally, will you for God's sake spit it out!

'Not who,' she repeated with laboured patience. 'Then…?'

'Boney.'

'Kenneth, I am understanding about one word in ten here…'

'Boney. He howls at night.'

'He's a dog? Boney's a dog. Yes?'

Pause.

'Not completely.'

'Kenneth, how can something be "not completely a dog"?'

'If he's dead love.'

'Boney's dead? Boney's a dead dog?'

A measured nod of assent from Kenneth, and the sliding of his gaze back to the floorshow.

'So,' Mel began, and suddenly felt strangely hilarious. 'So you're saying that Kelly hears the howling of a…'

'Ghost dog. Affirmative.'

'And you hear it too?'

He shrugged. 'On and off.' Yeah right, Mel thought.

'And June?'

'Oh June hears him.'

'And does anyone know why…?'

'June's got a theory.' Mel was starting to suspect that Kenneth's tone of voice was hiding something here. 'She thinks he's left something behind.'

'What, like a bone or something?' Mel wasn't able fully to control her own tone either. Was this another wind up?

'Chew toy. You know the kind of thing? Plastic bone with a squeaker in it. That's what he's looking for. According to June.'

'But if he's dead… I mean, this would have to be a spirit chew toy. Wouldn't it?'

Another shrug. 'No good asking me love. June's the expert. See according to June he's dead, but he doesn't know it yet. He hasn't moved on.'

'Because he hasn't found his chew toy?'

'Uhuh. That's why he has to keep on coming back.'

'Right. Right.' Mel nodded. 'And so the other night you, what, you chased him away? Boney?'

'I did.'

'How did he die?'

'Oh you know dogs,' Kenneth said, and, before Mel could pursue the point, stood. 'Want to see something?' Remembering this time to wince because of his bad back, he led the way into the garden. Mel followed and they both stood over a patch of lawn close to the patio: the turf was roughly torn away, the soil crumbly and black around it. Mel met Kenneth's eye enquiringly.

'It looks like it's been dug recently,' Mel said, turning over soil with her shoe.

'Yeah. Yeah it does doesn't it. Whenever we hear him we get a new hole.'

'You're saying…'

'He doesn't just howl. He digs.'

'So I see.'

'June says he's looking for it.'

'The chew toy.'

'Yeah.'

'Right.'

'You know, I had some trouble believing it at first. But the more it happens…'

'And there couldn't be any other explanation?'

'Like what?' Kenneth said, with a big you-tell-me face, and Mel was abruptly certain that Kenneth was up to something. Certain. Behind her back she felt the stilled presence of Kelly and the mute unnameable friend, synchronised conspirators.

14

Mel was sleeping over. She had her laptop open. Log entry. "Today was the ritual."

She was having trouble phrasing. She had to try to get the language right.

She stopped, her gaze wandering around Kelly's room. There were sounds from downstairs, voices in the kitchen, June and Kelly in some kind of inquisition. She met Dane's eye in Kelly's photograph, his scaffolder's hands dwarfing hers, glittering greedy eyes, hair-trigger vascularity. She could see something of Kenneth in that face, she thought; this could conceivably be Kenneth thirty years ago.

"...the ritual. Kenneth explained the purpose of it as follows. The dagger..." (this was Kenneth's word for the horrible rusty thing she had taken from Michael) "... belongs to him. It is his inheritance. He was bequeathed it through his father, whose father had given it to him, back for many generations. It dates back, in fact," (she worried over 'in fact', it seemed satiric somehow) "to Saxon times, when Kenneth's ancestors came to this site from their ancient kingdom, Cornwall, and began their exile. It is an ancient badge of kingship."

Badge of kingship. Kenneth had indicated that his kingly

name was in fact Marke (with an e): 'King Kenneth', though, had a certain ring to it, she thought. And why Mark-e anyway, she thought, unless it was German?

Mel recalled the moment in the back garden at sunset, the scruffy bonfire of skip-salvage and pallets, the smoke curling off away to the trees, the air trembling. Immediate family (though no sign of Kelly), plus Paulie, who had with him a girl of about ten. Music from the kitchen, June's choice, Celtic-sounding choral singing. The children moon-eyed and overtired. Catering by June, naturally: essentially anything that came in a bun or on a skewer, or that you could eat with your fingers. She kept a vigilant eye on things from the kitchen door, chain smoking.

"Kenneth made a speech."

Right. Well Kenneth had actually rambled on for the better part of ten minutes, about ancient prerogatives and blood debt, sacred land, time, dynasty. The ten year old girl with Paulie, long fair hair and very skinny arms, had taken a fancy to Mel. She had gazed solemnly up at her in the smoky light, her cheeks smudged, her nose running. Mel had felt the little fists bunching in her waist band as the planks crackled and popped.

The historical and racial details were somewhat imprecise. Kenneth's heritage wandered fairly freely between "Saxon" (a long time ago), "Mesolithic" (a very long time ago) and "Ancient" (before that, even). Saxon appeared to mean Nordic as well, and possibly even Viking, though also Celtic in places. Certainly June felt a strong Celtic connotation in all this. That final 'e', though, was puzzling however you thought about it.

But none of this was the point; today's proceedings were all about one single object, the dagger. Purifying it, because it had been polluted, by being touched by someone from outside the bloodline (i.e., Mel thought, me. Charming).

The item itself was laid on a trestle table next to Kenneth, along with some other bits and pieces of broken pottery and odd scraps of leather and fur, plus an object like a mildewed first-world-war flying helmet. These also were part of the 'birthright'. The twins stood close by: the covered one had a different duvet cover on, presumably, Mel thought, in honour of the occasion.

Kenneth stopped speaking, and picked up a large plastic washing up bowl. Something slopped over the edge as he lifted it, some liquid heavier and darker than water. In the uncertain light Mel couldn't be sure, but it certainly could have been blood. Kenneth put the bowl down again and immersed his hands in it, up to mid forearm. Then he raised both arms, and a slightly embarrassed cheer went up from Paulie. Kenneth flung the contents of the bowl onto the fire, and a thick evil smelling cloud rose up.

The unshrouded twin now took hold of the dagger and, with his shaky arm guided by Kenneth, approached the bonfire. He held it up to the flames.

Mel typed on. "Kenneth then made a short statement, concerning the properties of blood and fire. The dagger had now been purified, the wrath of dishonoured ancestors assuaged, and the land cleansed. The dagger could be returned to its place."

Kenneth and the twins went inside, and came back out a minute or two later, minus the dagger. Kenneth stopped to wash his hands and arms at the kitchen sink, June impassively smoking behind him.

And that was that. The group broke up shortly afterwards.

Mel pondered for a moment, her face gleaming with the reflected light of the laptop screen. How to convey the menace, the weirdness, the choking smoke and the flickering light, the sight of Kenneth elbow deep in gore, the ragged congregation, the serious faces? Kenneth, revealed now as some kind of ancestral chief, priest even, with the twins as acolytes?

And there was something else: at no point had Kenneth actually picked the thing up himself, and neither of the 'purifying elements' – the blood and the fire – had been allowed to touch it either, it remained as it had started out, rusty and stained. Funny kind of cleansing, Mel thought. Richard had said she could go directly to the Rationality Unit if she needed any specific guidance. She would, she decided, send them her account of Kenneth's ritual, just so her back was covered. Just in case.

"Further enquiry will be needed to establish some of the details with any precision," she wrote. Well that was certainly one way of saying it.

She went to the open window, the gingham curtains billowing gently. The night sky was an extraordinary azure, ghosts of light trailing along the horizon. A wisp of music, a tenor voice this time, heroic, turbulent, turning on the air. Hunting horns. Closer now. She breathed it in as it throbbed, ached, faded again.

She woke in the night to a sound from the garden. At the darkened window she watched as two tiny forms clambered over the shadowy fence from next door, one having some difficulty managing its duvet cover, the other clutching a bundle of some kind. They let themselves in the back door. Very silent. She glanced at her watch: three thirty. She duly logged the event. She was, she thought soberly, going to have to have a talk with the twins one day soon.

15

Bright and early next day she threw the curtains open and was confronted by the sight of Kelly being addressed by a short, aggressive-looking woman with complicated hair. Forty-odd, dressed in a polyester pants suit in burgundy and a cream blouse with a cravat in mauve. Another blinding day, the sun already strong and implacable. The woman was clearly giving Kelly a dressing down. Kelly stood meekly but also negligently as the woman spoke, one foot rotating through a few lazy degrees, back and forth. The woman then struck a pose, arms out, hands twisted into her face, her nails long and pointed. Kelly did it too, but with a couldn't-give-a-shit kind of face. Like this you mean?, her raised eyebrows said. Like this?

The woman (Mel tried to remember her name, June had told her, it was Kelly's dance teacher) took a few steps away and executed a move, arms flung out again, her face a twisted mask of expressivity. Kelly did it too, but in such a way as to strip it entirely of meaning. The woman was stony, professionally patient. Mrs. Slight: the architect in chief of Kelly's ambitions, the captain of the good ship Dance. Again. Like this. 5-6-7-8…

Mel caught Mrs. Slight on her way out.

'Hi! I wondered if you had a minute…?'

They sat in the kitchen, Mrs. Slight with her legs elegantly crossed, sipping from a glass of iced water. Kelly could be heard upstairs.

'I don't know if Kelly mentioned anything to you, or June,' Mel said by way of introduction. 'I'm working with the family too. For a couple of weeks.'

'June said something about it yes,' Mrs. Slight said, 'helping out with Kelly.' Mrs. Slight's voice was exact, but even in relaxation it carried a hint of something extra, a vibrancy, as if she might at any moment break into song, or, indeed, dance.

'Helping out. Precisely,' Mel said. 'Whatever I can do really. So I was wondering if I could talk to you about Kelly, how it's all going…?'

'I think of Kelly as one of my special girls,' Mrs Slight stated blankly, with no detectable flicker of irony, or even insistence. She merely stated it as a fact. 'Some girls have got it, some haven't. Kelly's got it.'

'Well you only have to watch her to see that,' Mel said.

'She needs work, of course. Everyone appreciates that. Raw talent like hers will only get you so far. It's a tough business. I've trained girls who've gone on to join contemporary dance troupes all over the world, West End, Europe. You name it. Cruises. But it's not all glitter and glamour as I never tire of telling them. You need that special something, that wow factor, so you stand out from all the other girls. If you're really going to make it. It's about channelling, focusing.'

'And I'd imagine support at home is important.'

'Oh absolutely critically important, yes,' Mrs. Slight said. 'It can be decisive.'

'You need people to believe in you.'

'Absolutely. But more importantly of course…'

'You need to believe in yourself?'

Mrs. Slight, perhaps a touch miffed to have been beaten to this well-chewed chicken nugget of showbusiness lore, continued. 'You must believe in your talent,' she said, as if correcting her.

'So I suppose June is a key player here?'

Judicious nodding. 'June has been a very supportive mother. She helps out a great deal with costumes and so on.'

Mel noted the limitations placed on this statement.

'But it's perhaps not June who's driving this on?'

'Kelly has been blessed in the shape of her step-father.'

'Kenneth?' Mel tried not to sound so surprised.

'Before Kenneth started to take an interest Kelly was nothing more than another starstruck girl with dreams and a lot to learn.'

'And now?'

'Well as you see. It's Kenneth who's organised her, got her into a regular routine. Kenneth sees to it that she makes all her classes, takes her examinations, rehearses. It was Kenneth, in fact, who suggested I take her under my wing a bit. Once he realised what she'd got.'

'But Kenneth... I mean, Kenneth doesn't know anything about dance does he?'

'Kenneth knows potential when he sees it. And so do I. It's something you can't train into people. You either have an eye or you don't. Kenneth is blessed.'

'So he contacted you? Initially?'

'Oh Kenneth and I go back forever,' Mrs. Slight said, shaking her head and gazing off into the distance, not wishing to be drawn.

'And Kelly's been in training for, how long?'

'She first came to me when she was eight, I think. Seven or eight.'

Mel controlled her face. Coughed. Six years?

'That shows some dedication,' she said evenly, and Mrs. Slight raised eyebrows.

'Kelly, to be absolutely candid with you, comes and goes in terms of her actual application to the discipline, the craft. Without Kenneth behind her...'

'So Kenneth has to push her a bit sometimes?'

'Kenneth is Kelly's rock. If only all of my girls had a Kenneth in their lives.'

Mel couldn't fail to hear the tone of voice here, even allowing for the distorting effects of the expressivity. Mrs. Slight and Kenneth eh? she thought. And they go way back do they?

'Ah here, if I'm not mistaken, is the man in question,' Mrs. Slight said, twisting round as a key turned in the front door. 'Kenneth! Your ears must have been burning.'

'Marise,' he said, and suffered himself to be kissed on each cheek.

'Kenny,' Mrs. Slight murmured, and pulled herself away.

'How's she going on?'

'Well. We'll try again on Thursday.' The day after tomorrow, Mel noted. How many lessons did poor Kelly have?

'Give you a lift somewhere?' Kenneth offered, and Mrs. Slight shook her head vigorously.

'But you can give me a hand getting it started.'

'You're not still trying to drive that bloody Volvo are you?' Kenneth said.

'So pleased to have met you,' she said, and gave Mel a stilted courtesy hug. 'Wiedersehen!' She linked her arm through Kenneth's as he walked her to the door. Mel could hear Kelly stamping about upstairs, arguing with June. Mrs. Slight's car made some unhealthy-sounding coughing and grinding before the motor caught.

Mel got her chance with the twins later that day. She happened to be passing their room, as Kelly happened to be coming out. Storming out, even. The door slammed hard, and Kelly vanished into her own room. Mel tapped on the twins' door. 'Guys? Have you got a minute? Is this a good time?'

There were bunk beds, with a ladder to the top, duvet covers and pillows with cartoon action heroes on them, two of everything, identical. Socks and plastic things all over the floor. Football posters on the walls. She left the door slightly open.

The boys were sitting on the bottom bunk, one as ever in full mufti.

'So, hi fellas,' she said, and was rewarded with attentive, if blank, looks from whoever was uncovered. 'Listen, I wanted to ask you something. OK?' She tried for a strictly-between-us tone, but there was no sign of any complicity. 'I need you to help me out.' She was aware of June moving about outside, humming aggressively. She lowered her voice, leaned in a bit closer.

'David?'

'My name...'

'Michael then. Michael?'

He assented, grudgingly. Maybe.

'Look, I wanted to ask you. Is it a game? With the duvet cover?' She gestured to David, who was mute beside him. 'Can you tell me about it?'

'It's his turn,' Michael said.

'You take it in turns? To wear it?'

Slow nodding. Michael's eyes were darting about all over the room. Very uncomfortable with this.

'What, he does it for an hour and then you do it?'

'Day.'

'He has to wear it for a whole day?'

Nodding.

'And then tomorrow it'll be you? And why can't he speak?'

'Not allowed to speak when you're covered.'

'Golly!' Mel said. 'Why ever not?'

'Rules,' Michael said briskly, and shrugged.

'So it's not always David covered up. Sometimes it's you?' She had suspected this. Nodding.

'Look, I've got to ask you,' she said in her most animated tone. 'I mean, why?'

'Rules. Dane told us.'

'What do you mean, honey?'

'Rule of silence,' Michael murmured, and Mel craned in closer to hear him.

'Sorry? Say it again?'

A breathless giggle from beside him.

'Sweetheart, I can't quite understand what you're saying…' she whispered, when June bustled in to break it up.

'Oh sorry love, I need to get these towels out of here. Stinking the place up,' she said, all cheerful busyness. Mel felt the moment slip away.

'Right. Well, see you fellas,' she said, and stood to leave. The twins remained impassive. She heard June chirruping behind her.

16

Waiting for her at home was a letter.

The Rationality Unit,
an executive agency of
The Office of the Deputy Prime Minister.
Date as postmark

Dear Ms. Banff,

We are in receipt of your letter.

A clear and unambiguous distinction is to be drawn between the 'religious' and the 'irrational'.

Bona fide religious beliefs must be respected, and under no circumstances must the free expression of them (unless injurious to others) be in anyway impeded. European human rights legislation is explicit in this regard (see for example, Department of the Home Office v Goscinski 1994), and is incorporated in UK law.

Irrational beliefs, however, can and must be challenged. Irrational beliefs would include, though by no means be limited to, the following:

1. The Supernatural. This would include such phenomena as

ghost sightings, ouija board use, poltergeist manifestations, waking dreams, messages from 'the other side' etc.

2. The Inexplicable. Here we would include any assertions which cannot be validated. Miraculous healing, spirit healing, (but see below), and any non-standard procedure or ritual whose purpose is healing should all be challenged, on the basis that there is no reliable evidence for their efficacy. As a rule of thumb, any procedures which are not offered by the NHS will fall into this category. (NB: Homeopathy, therapeutic massage and other alternative remedies are increasingly offered by GPs. Such treatments should therefore be regarded as valid, but only when offered through a GP or other recognised medical professional.)

Also included here would be any reported incidents which violate known physical laws, such as: clairvoyance, astral projection, past life memory, astrological predictions, premonitions, prophecy, divination etc. (NB: Many, if not most, of the above are core components of many major religious systems, and thus should be regarded as valid in that context only. The inexplicable and the supernatural also play important roles in many major religions. Where an irrational belief of this kind is a substantive or significant component of a well-established and rule-governed religious belief system (see attached schedule), then such beliefs should be regarded as valid.

Your account raises questions in other areas, and I have passed your comments on, where appropriate, to the relevant agencies.

We hope this clarifies the present position.

Yours sincerely,

T. Collinge,
Rationality Unit, Field Response Group.

17

Next day, Mel collared June at the airing cupboard.

'So June. I was wanting to get things straight in my head.'

'Yes love.' June was arranging pastel-coloured sheets on slatted shelves.

'It's really about Kelly's father.'

June stiffened.

'I'll tell you about Kelly's father shall I? Kelly's father was a bad man who told lies and got what was coming to him. He told lies to me, he told lies to the police.'

'Lies? What kind of lies?'

June sighed.

'What you mean you haven't got it all written down?'

Mel could not fail to detect bitterness here.

'June, if you'd rather not talk about Gary...'

'See?' June said, 'I knew you'd have it written down somewhere. You being so orderly and everything.'

Mel did indeed have it written down. Gary Chope was currently under psychiatric supervision having been the subject of an attack of quite extraordinary viciousness 12 months ago, in the course of which he sustained severe facial injuries, most notably the partial removal – hacking off – of his nose. Mel had it written down because Kenneth had been questioned by Sussex Police about the incident. Kenneth had been named by Gary as one of the assailants, a charge he flatly denied, producing an alibi which effectively ruled him out of the enquiry. This had all taken place at roughly this time last year, during Dane's visit to the Medcrupps. Dane had also been questioned, but he too had an alibi. There was no physical evidence, although Gary had told police of a knife, a blade...

'He was a different man when I knew him. He was a lovely man actually. He had some problems of course. Who hasn't eh? There were drugs and he got the anxieties, self-harming and that, running out in his pants, you know the kind of thing love. But a more caring man you couldn't wish to meet. Oh he was lovely in those days. Then when Kelly came on the scene everything changed. I won't lie to you darling, Kelly wasn't what you call planned. She just kind of happened. Then I met Kenneth. Then Gary started playing up really bad. More drugs – he started jabbing speed. More rows. Wouldn't help with nappies or bathtime, stayed out all day in the pub. Stopped working. If it hadn't been for Kenneth I don't know what I'd have done. It was rough for a while love. Gary I lost track of. He went away. He said he wanted to see Kelly a few times, but he only upset her and Kenneth stopped it. He drifted away.'

'Until last year?'

June sighed again.

'God knows what made him do it. But here he was back again, wanting to see Kelly. He was hanging round outside for a while. I found her talking to him once, told him to get on his bike. He was off his head mostly. Kenneth saw him off a couple of times. Then he pushed a letter through the door, says Kelly is in danger.'

'And then...'

'And then he gets himself into a ruck outside a pub. It was a drug thing if you ask me. He wasn't always too careful who he dealt with was Gary, and he was fairly messy at this point. I think he must have pissed someone off on a drug deal, and they got him. Police didn't think that though, which shows you what they know about anything.'

'They suspected Kenneth?'

'First suspect love. Gary told them.'

'So why did Gary blame Kenneth?'

'You tell me. Bitter probably. About me. Wanted me back maybe? Thought he could fit Kenneth up with the police, get him out the way. I mean Kenneth's no angel, he's known to the police, as they say. Well as you know.'

Mel nodded. Kenneth did indeed have something of a history with Sussex Police, though he hadn't been successfully charged with anything since the 1970's. Her thoughts turned to Kenneth's Saxon dagger.

'And Dane…?'

'Oh Dane. Well what you need to understand about Dane is that he's never had a real relationship with his father, Kenneth's brother. He's always been one of Kenneth's special boys. Dane looks up to Kenneth. And Kenneth says he wishes Dane was his own lad. Dane's spent a few summers here and him and Kenneth always got on. He'd run errands for Kenneth, that kind of thing, help him out with business and that, you know all the king-in-exile stuff. He'd do anything for Kenneth.'

'But Dane was questioned by police as well?'

'Well that's what Gary told them didn't he? He said Dane and Kenneth jumped him. Said Dane threatened him with a knife, then stabbed him, then Kenneth bit him, if you please, while Dane held him down, then Dane stabbed him a bit more and cut off his nose! I mean!'

June was chewing her lip.

'Look darling. I know you're here to help, and we all appreciate it, really we do. But I've got Kelly to see about. She doesn't know what happened to her dad. Gary. As far as she's concerned he might as well be dead. Ancient history. Dane must have let slip something about the nose though, cos she has nightmares. You should hear her. Kenneth says it'll pass in time. You're not to say anything to her. You won't will you?'

'June? Do you mind if I ask you something?'

'Anything you like love.'

'Are you frightened of Gary? That he'll come back?'

June heaved up a huge sigh.

'There's a lot of things scare me darling.'

'Boney?'

'It's not Boney that bothers me. Not as such. I mean he was only a dog. Ghost dog, what harm can he do really?'

'Whose dog was he? Kenneth's?'

'Gary's dog love. When Gary came back last year he had this dog with him. Then before the incident, dog turns up dead, in our back yard. Head half hacked off. It was horrible. We reckoned Gary must have done it to scare us. Didn't know what to do about it. So we buried him.'

'In the back yard?'

June nodded.

'Kenneth saw to it. And then it all started up. The howling at night, my love. The holes. No-one knew what to make of it. Kelly's been at her wits' end. But it's not only the dog.'

'What else then?'

'Think about it. Ghost dog, he's going to have a ghost master isn't he. That's what's eating at Kelly. See, she knows something's up with her dad, but she doesn't know what. She thinks he's dead too maybe. Maybe he's coming back, for her. Maybe Boney's his harbinger.'

'Sorry, his…?'

'An avatar love. An aspect of his spirit self, an annuncio.'

'You're losing me June…'

'It's complicated.' June shook her head, her eyes wandering over the slatted shelves.

'And what do you think?'

'I think the dead walk, sweetie. I think Gary could be dead. He's not finished with us, that's what I think.'

'Is this why you don't like going out these days June?'

'I need to be here. To watch. And I need to look after Kelly.'

'Kelly says she's looking after you.'

'We see to each other. When Kenneth's away there's no-one. We've only got each other.'

'June, I don't know if this has got anything to do with it, but do you know why the twins dress the way they do?'

'Oh.' She laughed, a quick breathless snort. 'Well I'll tell you love. It started last year when Dane was here last.'

'Something Dane said to them?'

'Must be. He's a joker is Dane. Probably spun them some fairy story. They'll grow out of it.'

'It doesn't worry you?'

'Love, I've got that much on my plate, and it's not harming anyone is it.'

'What about school?'

'Oh they don't like school very much.'

'June. See, you know why I'm here don't you? To help you?'

Slow nodding, but June's attention had wandered.

'And to help you I need to understand you first. And I'm worried that I'm not, not really. Nothing's really getting any clearer. It gets murkier and murkier to be honest. Nothing seems to make sense.'

Nothing back from June.

'I mean, what am I going to say in my report? How do I explain anything?'

Deep sighs.

'How do you see things turning out June? Are you optimistic about the future?'

Slow shake of the head. Mel was alarmed to note June's eyes start to swim. She fingered away a tear.

'It'll get worse before it gets better...'

'Is there anything else you can tell me June?' Mel asked as gently, as persuasively as she knew how. 'Anything at all?'

'I've got things to see to,' June said abruptly, and was gone. Mel remained staring at the neatly folded bedding.

Mel was leaving for the day when she popped her head round Kelly's door and saw Kelly and June busily occupied with a dress fitting. The wedding dress, minus its train now, hanging somewhat limply on Kelly's spare frame, expertly set off by a baseball cap with a gauzy veil and high-heeled trainers, all in gleaming white, with Adidas stripes.

June stood, and Mel took Kelly in. She was bridal.

'We were just trying it on her,' June said quickly, looking trapped. 'She's the right height and shape and everything.'

Mel smiled.

'Oh by the way, in case you forgot,' she said. 'Tomorrow is the weekly group discussion. You got the agendas didn't you?' June smiled tightly.

'Four o'clock,' Mel said, and left.

18

Faith Community Liaison Group
Rapid Response Team
Date as postmark.

Dear Ms. Banff,
We are in receipt of your letter, which was forwarded to us by the Rationality Unit.

The use of animal products in ritual observance is an area which, in our estimation, would need to be evaluated from the twin perspectives of health and safety, and animal welfare. Your comments will be passed on to the appropriate departments.

Yours sincerely,

Ms. M. Quelp
FCLG Information Directorate

19

'Jamie…'

'Hm…?'

'What's a harbinger?'

'A what?'

'Harbinger.'

'One who comes before.'

'Before what?'

'Whatever comes after. Obviously. Duh.'

'Great. Great help there Jamie. Annuncio?'

'One who announces.'

'What, like an announcer then?'

'Yeah but not like train cancellations. This is poncier. For poncy announcements. You know, incarnations, immaculate conceptions, that kind of area.'

'Great. Avatar?'

He put his paper down.

'Mel, who have you been talking to, Madame Blavatsky?'

'June.'

'Ah. I see. Well, let's think now. An avatar is, I think, a manifestation.'

'Of…?'

'Any kind of spirit entity. God, prophet, that kind of thing.'

'Ghost?'

'I don't see why not.'

'Ghost dog?'

He shrugged.

'In Juneworld, Mel, I sense that more or less anything is possible. Avatar is also sometimes a kind of special version of the thing itself. Or it's one aspect of the thing. Or whatever.'

'June said aspect. But what aspects have dogs got?'

'June's the expert. Why not ask her? Maybe one aspect's barking, another one's chasing after sticks…'

'Digging?'

'Well obviously. This is, of course, the big unspoken story about gardening, the havoc wreaked by the digging avatars of dead dogs…'

'Also he howls.'

'I probably would if I was him. I think June might make me howl. How did he die anyway?'

'Kenneth won't say.'

'You see, if it was a violent end, he might be returning to be avenged.'

'Kenneth says he's looking for his squeaker.'

'Or that of course. Certainly. You can see what a powerful motivator that might be.'

'Ah well,' Mel sighed and stretched luxuriously, wriggling her toes. 'All will become clear.'

'You want to put money on that?'

20

Despite the unrelentingly gorgeous weather, family conferences had to be held indoors, in deference to June, so they sat in the kitchen. Mel made sure everyone had their agendas and then called the meeting to order.

'Now before we begin our discussion, has anyone got any questions about anything?'

'Yeah I have.' Kenneth, inevitably, with his hand up, like at school. Mel sighed.

'Yes Kenneth?'

'It's about that thing about Socrates.'

'The syllogism. Yes.'

'Can't fail, you reckon?'

'Uhuh. You can only get right answers. It won't let you go wrong.'

'Right I see. So all a's are b, c is an a, so therefore...'

'Exactly'

'C is a b.'

'Right.'

'So for instance, all men are mortal...'

'That's it.' (Beaming) 'You've got it exactly. Understand that and you understand all. Well nearly.'

'Infallible you say.'

Solemn nodding

'Can't go wrong.'

'So let's try it out. You are a social worker…'

'OK.'

'All social workers are lesbians…'

'Yeees…'

'So therefore, you are…'

'Wait wait wait. It only works if the things you plug into it are true.'

'So you're telling me you're not a lesbian?'

'No, I'm telling you that the syllogistic method only gives true answers if the premises are themselves true.'

'You sound a bit like a lesbian there, to be honest love… Anyway, I thought the method was infallible. Now you're telling me it can produce wrong answers.'

'It is infallible, but…'

'But only if you already know what's true in the first place.'

'Yes but…'

'So it can't tell the difference between true statements and untrue statements…'

'Well no, only an assessment of the evidence will do that.'

'So I find out the truth about something, and then your big-shot method comes along and tells me it's true, except you can't be sure, and it could equally well be false…'

'No no no no no.' (Yes.) 'Look, Kenneth if you feed in false premises, it will generate a false but logically rigorous response…' She felt herself floundering. 'The truth value… Look, the truth value of the premises…'

'So you're telling me you've never even thought about it?'

'What?'

'You. And another woman.'

'Kenneth, can I say, I'd rather you didn't…'

'That's not very nice is it Kenneth?' June said. 'How am I supposed to teach the twins about nice funny and nasty funny if you go on like that?'

Kenneth made a mock salute and sat back. He hadn't finished yet.

'OK. Look. All men are mortal. See, thing is, though, you've already said all men are mortal, so Socrates must be mortal mustn't he? If he's a man? You don't need the… what do you call it…'

'Syllogism.'

'Yeah. Don't need it at all, it doesn't add anything to what you've already got. See, your first statement is really "all men, including Socrates, are mortal". The end. Seems to me you've already assumed what you're trying to prove. Wouldn't you say?'

Begging the question, it was called. A rudimentary error in logic. Kenneth folded his arms and raised enquiring eyebrows. Mel could imagine Jamie's pedantic voice saying this, pleased with itself, finding a flaw. Where was Kenneth getting it from, Mel wondered wildly. And was he right? Were there really problems in the syllogistic method? Because if that was true…

'Right well, anyway let's move along,' she said, briskly consulting her agenda paper. 'You all remember the rules from the briefings don't you? Only one person to speak at a time, no interruptions, questions to go through the chair – me – and respect each other's contributions even when you disagree. Alright? Now you'll see that the subject for discussion today is "What is the future of the Royal Family?" Who'd like to start?'

Shifting of limbs. Kenneth cracked some knuckles, then tore a strip off his agenda and chewed it. June gazed into space and sighed. The sun poured through the window and open door in solid blocks, wafting in smells of cut grass and flowering privet and hot earth, while music thumped and paused and thumped again from an open window a few doors down.

'June? What about you?'

June stirred. 'Good luck to them if that's what they want to do then they should get on and do it shouldn't they? I'm not stopping them am I?' she said, and, as if exhausted by the effort of this non-impedance of royalty, slumped back.

'So you're, broadly speaking, in favour of them continuing?'

'Yeah well it doesn't much matter what I think does it?'

'But June, that's what this is all about.'

'Oh you're going to go off and tell them are you? Don't worry Your Majesty, I've talked to June and she thinks you should carry on?'

'No but June, if we're going to discuss it then we need to know what we all think about it. Don't we?' June shrugged. 'Well alright. Kenneth?'

'Royal Family, stay or go?'

'In a nutshell. Exactly.'

'Not our decision to take.'

'Really,' Mel said, with a hugely encouraging gesture of fascination, her face a furrowed field of interest. 'You don't think we should even talk about it?'

'Talk about anything you like. But Royal Family, they've got a right, that's all there is to it. It's not for you to say.'

'A right?'

'Right of Kingship.'

'Interesting,' Mel said, nodding slowly. 'So, in your opinion...'

'I've said my opinion haven't I.' Kenneth, clearly, had said all he had to say on the subject. He had spoken.

'OK then. Great. So, Kelly?'

Kelly was in wistful hair-twining mode. 'I think if they've got that much money they should give it away,' she said finally. Her voice was slow as honey. 'To poor people. People who haven't got anything at all.'

'Wonderful,' Mel said brightly. 'Thanks Kelly. Right, well how about if we take each argument in turn…'

'That's typical. Isn't that typical June?' Kenneth said, drowning her out. Mel made a mental note of the swift and immediate resort to the personal, the attack *ad hominem*. 'Everything should be for nothing. Isn't that right Kelly? Stands to reason, everyone should give you all their money. Of course they should.' Imputation of base motive, Mel thought. Crude but effective.

'Through the chair please Kenneth…'

'I didn't mean me…' Kelly started, but was shouted down again.

'Why should they give you their money? What's in it for them?' Kenneth demanded, smiling, bristling, bullying.

'Kelly?'

'Yeah well it's no good talking to him, is it?'

'But isn't that a reasonable point?' Mel persisted, sensing an opening for a discussion of the workings of the tax and welfare system here. Kelly, clearly, sensed no such opportunity.

'Oh yeah take his side.'

'Kelly, no-one's taking sides…'

'You're always doing it.'

'Watch your lip madam.' This helpful interjection from June. Mel battled on.

'I meant, Kelly, what if someone said to you, you should give me your money because you've got more than me. Would you do it?'

'Any road, genius,' Kenneth barged in, 'if they gave you all their money, you'd be richer than them wouldn't you? So you'd have to give it all back again. According to you.' The *reductio ad absurdum*, sudden, merciless and lethal. Kenneth's teeth were glinting, Mel noted.

'Smelly,' came a tiny voice from Mel's left, and the twins were suddenly convulsed. Kelly stood and, uttering something scalding about immaturity, absented herself noisily from the meeting.

'Anyway,' June said reflectively into the silence, 'he's Greek isn't he? Prince Charles?'

'Charles?' Mel said, completely thrown. 'No, Philip surely. The Duke of Edinburgh.'

'No the other one with the ears. Greek. I read it in the paper.'

Was this, Mel wondered briefly, the moment to raise the issue of evaluating the trustworthiness of sources? She opened her mouth.

'I've got a question. For the group.' Kenneth's voice. Of course. She sat back again.

'Yes Kenneth.'

'This is all about being reasonable, right?'

'Absolutely.'

'So my question is, what's reasonable?'

'Well, it's what a reasonable person would consider to be – '

'Reasonable.'

'Yes, but...'

'So it's whatever you think?'

'If I'm reasonable, yes.'

'What if you're not though. What if you think you are but you're not? You'd have no way of knowing would you? Except by using your reason, which is the exact thing that would have gone wrong.'

'Kenneth, I think we might be wandering away slightly here...'

June stood abruptly and muttered something about having a word with madam upstairs.

'So it's just you and me,' Kenneth said.
'And the twins.'
'Let's see how reasonable they are. Shall we? Lads? What do you think? Should we have the boring old queen, or should your dad be king of everything forever instead?'
'King of everything!' a voice came back, and the boys were immediately aroused, leaping and flailing their arms around, screaming like chimps. 'King of everything!'
'See? They know what's what, my boys,' Kenneth said and, toppling back in his chair as the twins flung themselves at him, grappled them both to the floor where they writhed in ticklish delirium. 'So. How many points we got this week then?' he said, with a twin pinned and wriggling under each arm, and Mel raised her eyebrows and emitted a puff of air.
'Ah well,' she said, arranging her papers. 'This might be a good moment to adjourn the meeting…'
The doorbell rang, there was a commotion from the stairs, then some screaming from the front door, followed by a long tumultuous silence. Kenneth met Mel's eye. She was about to go and investigate when Kelly pushed the kitchen door open, a shy but triumphal smile lighting up her face. She was holding hands with someone behind her, pulling them in, and Mel knew who it was immediately, seconds before his head and neck and shoulders followed Kelly into the doorway. He stood bobbing behind her and Kelly gazed up at him and then back at Mel. Eyes like plates.
'It's my cousin Dane,' she said.

June.

21

It rained for a week. Mel arrived to find Whitehawk swaddled in mist and drizzle, visibility abruptly reduced to zero. Footfalls were muted and sounds fell short, dogs barked fretfully from one end of the estate to the other, cars refused to start; padded buggies squeaked past, their plastic hoods fully engaged, tiny puckered faces inside like pissed-off baby astronauts in overgrown space helmets. The place was, if anything, less real than before, Mel thought, gazing out of her windscreen as she gathered herself for the coming visit. Less substantial.

That afternoon Dane and Kenneth had a meeting, in the shed. Mel watched from the kitchen as Dane trudged down the grey dripping garden and knocked on the door.

He was in there for a good two hours, while June and Kelly took turns to peer out of the kitchen window. At one point they heard a disturbance, something being knocked over, and June's hand tightened on Kelly's arm. Dane re-emerged, ducking his head on the shed doorway, and came back up the garden, licking his lips, tugging at his sweatshirt hood, kicking the mud. Halfway down he lifted his arms and folded his hands behind his head: surrender.

June had taken to disappearing into her bedroom for long sessions with the sewing machine. Mel heard the whine and stop, whine and stop at all times of the day and night. Some singing. She was also doing a lot of healing at the moment; women appeared and disappeared from her room at unexpected times. Mel understood that the technique of past-life healing involved crystals and a car battery; she was, she knew, going to have to discuss the science behind it with June at some point.

Sleepover.

Mel lay on Kelly's bed and considered her journal. She was attempting a profile of Dane. She wasn't, she felt, getting to the heart of it.

The first thing to note, the most significant thing, was that Dane was not actually resident at number 23; he was officially staying with June's sister Theresa on another part of the estate. But his first action was to take over the sofa bed from Paulie, who was dislodged, with some obvious sense of grievance according to June, back to his own place. Dane's sofa arrangements were on a scale Paulie had never attempted, involving not merely pillows and duvet but also a zone around the sofa itself where he kept essential items like remote controls and beer-can-ash-trays and a small heap of clothes and keys. He scratched and grimaced, he had pains in his stomach, he needed care.

All of which mess ought, of course, to have incurred the wrath of June, but, Mel noted, did not. On the occasion of her visit that day she had been let in by June, half-crouching, urgently murmuring about not waking him. The front room was still dark, unaired, smelling of ashtrays and beer, the TV a huge gleaming dusty shadow. June all but tiptoed past the commandeered sofa, navigating with elaborate care around a foot sticking out.

Dane was, clearly, disinclined to early rising; noon came and went and he slept on. One o'clock.

'He's shattered, poor love,' June said as she and Mel sat trying not to make any noise in the kitchen. Mel was administering a mathematical reasoning test; June was performing badly, getting no points, and looking generally distracted. 'I'll give him a shout in a minute. Take him some tea...' Mel heard a tone she couldn't remember hearing before in June's voice, nests and cotton wool and warm milk, a purring. If a is greater than x... Mel stopped. Hearts first.

'So! Bit of a surprise then, him (no questions as to who "him" referred to) turning up like this. Isn't it? You weren't expecting him were you?'

'There's always a place here for Dane,' June said, all throat, all dovecote. 'Always has been, always will be. Dane knows that.'

June was smoking heavily, it was affecting her voice, and she suddenly needed to lie down. Her feet, Mel noted, made barely a whisper on the deep living room carpet.

Ten minutes later, Mel heard coughing from the couch and, sensing her opportunity, reached for her Kui/Varney kit.

22

Baseline Assessment:
Dane King, (19), DOB: 3/10/84 Conducted by M Banff.

'OK Dane. I want to ask you a couple of questions, and you say true or false.'

He took a vast, bottomless pull on his smoke, then held, held, ah God, his head hung back, fell forward. Aaaaaah.

'Dane? We could do this another time...'

A shake of the head. Snap to rights. Bang on it. Give it me. Big breath out. Big grin.

'Go. Go.'

'OK.' Mel smiled a nervy smile. 'OK. Dane. All donkeys have four legs. Dobbin is a donkey. Therefore Dobbin has four legs.'

'True. Gimme.'

'Alright then. If all donkeys have four legs, and Dobbin has got four legs, then Dobbin is a donkey.'

'False. Come on.'

'And why false?'

'Because you didn't say only donkeys have four legs. Dobbin could be some other thing that's got four legs. Giraffe, let's say. Or a table.'

'A – sorry…?'

'Table's got four legs hasn't it? Dobbin's a table. No I got it, a darts tournament.' Dane brought out a hand from the duvet and scratched his forearm vigorously, frowning down at the elbow. Mel, distracted by the image of a darts tournament called Dobbin, was struck unexpectedly by his colouring, not ginger, not red; pale gold. His arm and wrist, and indeed his fingers and knuckles, and in fact all of him as far as she could see (which was quite far enough), were covered in gold hair. Or was it more like brass? He had the kind of skin that would burn streaky red immediately in the sun, until the freckles all joined up. He had a chunky identity bracelet on, Mel noted, and a matching neck chain, both in gold. Sweat rolled in his folds. He reached down to scratch at his ankle, the duvet moved, and Mel, unwittingly, discovered simultaneously that his preference was for sleeping *au naturel*, and that the gold hair was indeed distributed all over him. The jewellery was all, seemingly, that he slept in, nor did he seem exactly shy about it. Not ginger, she found herself saying, and couldn't help but wonder to whom and why. His colouring in fact, she thought, matched perfectly the door-furniture upstairs, which was 'gold-coloured'. So? He scratched more, and she again saw slightly further than she was comfortable seeing. She shook her head. Objectives, Protocols, Methodologies… She summoned up a professional manner.

'OK then Dane! Now, I toss a coin ten times, and it comes up heads each time; so the next throw…'

'False.'

'I haven't said it yet…'

'False anyway.' He yawned strenuously. 'You can't say anything about the next one. Each toss is independent. Chances are fifty/fifty, heads/tails every time. Or,' leaning in, finger pointing, 'or Dobbin with the four legs could be code for two blokes stitched together, like the Nazis...'

'Right. OK,' Mel said, shifting herself away, but smiling, 'one more. Now, if all squirrels like nuts, and Sammy doesn't...'

'...or he could be a collector of legs.'

Mel paused. Dane raised his eyebrows and lounged back in his snuggled nest, reaching behind his head for cigarettes and lighter. Cropped hair, crinkly eyes narrowed to slits, big dirty smile. He was what Mel's (alcoholic) mother would call 'a cheeky monkey'.

'A what?' Mel said, alert as ever for a Medcrupp-style wind-up. 'A collector of...?' Dane was unmistakeably Kenneth's relation, not June's. He lit the cigarette and got comfy again, tapping the ash into a nearby glass. To go with the gold colouring, Mel noted, were deep green eyes, severely shadowed, and a generally greenish complexion. He was, she thought, as if seen under water. He smiled a lot. There was something reptilian about the lids and the creases of the eyes, or perhaps it was even further back than that, amphibian maybe.

'Dobbin,' Dane said. 'He could be someone who collects legs. Artificial legs? He's maybe selling them on eBay or it makes his dick hard, you know he gets off on wheelchairs and callipers and that?'

'Right...'

'And he hasn't been collecting long has he, so he's only got the four. Legs. For now. Or...'

'Well Dane.' Mel had had enough variants on hypothetical four-leg-possessing entities for the moment, and smiled neutrally, putting her Kui/Varney materials back into the box. 'I think that's probably plenty for the time being...'

'Did I win?'

'It isn't really that kind of test.'

'That's what you think. You going to be here long, are you?'

128

'For a while.' She felt bold suddenly, reckless even. She wiped sweat from her cheeks. 'What about you?'

'For a while.' He folded his brawny arms behind his head and grinned inappropriately at her from his fragrant, snaggled mess of bedding. Belch. 'Yeah. Definitely.'

Aggregate score: 0.86.

0.86.

Mel checked her figures again, but there it was. Dane had the logical functioning of the average veterinarian student. He was, in fact, already slightly ahead of the average mortgage advisor (0.82), army NCO (0.79), or middle-ranking health manager (0.77). He was intellectually equipped to run a theme pub. He could supervise electrical work on railways. He was, comfortably, in the top quartile of the population. Mel sat back and pondered.

'Dane King is Kenneth's nephew, through Kenneth's brother Malcolm. Dane's parents, Malcolm and Alice King, live in Tintagel, Cornwall, where they run a bed and breakfast hotel and tea-shop. Dane is the oldest of four children. He has spent much of his time with Kenneth and June in Whitehawk, having first run away there at the age of eleven. Dane has no particular animosity against his natural parents or home, beyond the observation that "it's a bit boring." Kenneth and June have acted as part-time surrogate parents to Dane over the last eight years. Dane has assisted Kenneth in the running of his business.'

Mel stopped and considered.

'Dane's position in the household is, however, by no means clear. He has no room of his own, for instance, and there are some indications that Kenneth may be less pleased by his arrival than June, or, say…'

Mel allowed a memory to come into her head. Late afternoon, the mist had finally melted away to reveal a sulky grey overcast sky and stoking temperatures. From the bathroom window she saw Kelly practising in the back garden, and something was different, immediately, obviously different. Mel came down to the open kitchen door to find Dane, stretched out smoking on a recliner on the patio, lobster-baked, while Kelly danced.

But that was the point, Mel had thought, watching Dane watching Kelly. She was *dancing* now.

23

Dane was ill. The couch became a sick bed, anxiously attended by June at every moment, the room a gloomy malodorous place. Mel stooped and whispered. He complained of fever, nausea, weakness in the legs. There was a bad smell around him. Kelly hovered nearby, slyly.

And next day Mel found, near his head, a plug of some kind of leaf matter. Bitter smelling, it left a deep bluish smear on the pillow. She removed it as gently as she could, and realised, with some relief, that she would have to say something about this now. It had become a clear cut health and safety issue.

'June, I'm wondering if maybe Dane shouldn't see a doctor?' she said as June tidied away some detritus from around the couch where Dane stirred uneasily, occasionally moaning gently, from a dark dream. 'It's been two days now, and he doesn't seem to be improving.'

'It'll get worse before it gets better,' June said darkly.

'June, now you know I'm not here to interfere. But I'm a tiny bit worried about Dane. I was wondering if you knew what this was…?' She produced the plug of folded leaves, and June sat back and exhaled smoke very deliberately. 'I found it on the couch,' Mel added, and awaited an answer.

'Dane's one of ours,' June said finally, and Mel tilted her head: don't understand. 'Dane's with us. We do things a certain way round here.'

'June, I'm sorry but I have to ask, have you attempted to heal Dane somehow?'

June shook her head slowly, but there was a reservation, and Mel's peripheral vision found Kelly loitering in the doorway, white with anxiety.

'Kelly?'

'OK Kelly, now I'm going to ask you questions and you're going to tell me the exact truth, OK? Serious now?'

Kelly nodded.

'Because I have statutory obligations here, Kelly. Do you know what that means?' Mel said. Kelly shook no, giggled. 'It means that I can get into trouble, real trouble, if I don't do my job properly.' Kelly shrugged, bit at a corner of a fingernail. Twisted on a toe. Young, Mel thought, young for fourteen.

'Have you or anyone in the house used any kind of alternative or complementary therapy on Dane?' Nodding. 'Yes? Who? You?'

Nodding.

'So can you tell me exactly what? Sweetie, Dane might be sicker than you realise. You've got to tell me what you've given him.'

'Leaves.'

'What, these?' Mel showed her the folded batch. 'What are they?'

'It's only a laugh really.'

'I don't think Dane's enjoying it very much. What have you given him?'

'My mum give it me. She said she uses it on Kenneth sometimes. If he can't... you know.'

'You mean an aphrodisiac?'

'My mum calls it love potion number nine. But it's only a laugh really…'

'Kelly, you're not… Kelly, I can't believe…' Mel was struggling for a response. 'You're fourteen years old for God's sake, what do you know about medicine?'

'My mum taught me. She knows. Ask anyone. She mostly does past life healing.'

'Sorry, past…?'

'If you were sick. In one of your past lives. My mum can heal that. And I can do things too. She's taught me. So I give him a decoction.'

'A what?'

Kelly pouted: don't you know nothing?

'Leaves. You make a paste and steep it in hot water, then he drinks it.'

Herbal tea, too sweet, with a nagging aftertaste, like old coins in the mouth, like blood…

'Kelly, Dane is getting worse, surely you can see that? Don't you think you might have poisoned him?'

'Not if you do it right.'

'Kelly I'm going to have to insist that we get a doctor out to Dane right away. Do you understand?' Mel was breathing hard. She put a hand to her chest.

'Doctor,' Kelly said contemptuously, and sniffed. Mel took her wrist.

'Yes, Kelly, a doctor, you know? Like on Holby City?'

'Do what you like. It'll get worse before…'

'I'm not listening to you anymore Kelly,' Mel said, and stood. 'And look, Kelly. Be careful. You know what I'm talking about, don't you?' Kelly raised her eyebrows: do I?

Dane was back on his feet by mid-afternoon, though he was still weak and his eyes were bloodshot, and his complexion paler green than before. He was moved out onto the patio, his needs and whims closely attended to by June, who was even prepared to come right outside to bring him cups of tea, ashtrays, snacks and so on, all placed within a lazy arm's reach on a small table beside him. Kelly was keeping out of the way. Whatever it was, it had passed.

24

Debate. 15/7/03. Chaired by M. Banff. Present…
Oh skip it. Mel licked her lips. She read aloud:

'Yesterday was a big day for asthma sufferers in Southern India. According to astrologers, sardines smeared with special herbs which are eaten on that day will effect a miraculous cure. Tens of thousands of asthmatics from all over the sub-Continent attended the ceremony in Hyderabad. The cure is distributed free by the Goud family, who, they claim, were given the secret of the remedy by a Hindu saint in the 1860s. Despite demands from the Indian Medical Association for the cure to be made public so that it can be subjected to scientific scrutiny, the family have always insisted on maintaining the secret, fearing that it would be "commercialised" if revealed. The Goud family claim they were warned that the remedy would cease to work if it were made public.

'Right,' Mel said, 'so what do we think of that? Does that raise any questions in anyone's mind?'

'I wonder what the herbs are they're using?' June said after a short pause. 'I could do with something reliable for asthma…'

'June, I was thinking more about the story as a whole really. For instance, the date to do this on has to be chosen by astrologers. What do we think about that?'

'Well it's amazing isn't it, how they know the right day… '

'What she means, June,' Dane said, 'is that it all sounds a bit dodgy.'

'Well I was going to say, is that how we do things here? Do doctors prescribe secret fish on special days or whatever?'

'I can't say I've ever tried live fish myself…' said June. 'But if it works…'

'That bloke in Shoreham harbour could probably get them for you,' Kenneth said. 'I'll have a word…'

'Ah. Aha,' Mel jumped in, a sentence late, 'if it works. But does it? You see, when you're reading something, it's terribly important to be aware that it may be saying something more than just the words themselves…'

'Don't get you love.'

'Well for instance. The last line of the article, about how the cure would stop working if it was commercialised.'

'Yeah…

'Well you could say the same thing quite differently: you could say that if the cure was properly scrutinised it would be shown to be a fake.'

'You think it's a fake?'

'Well what does anyone else think? Does anyone think it's true? About the fish?'

'Hundreds of thousands of people in India seem to think so,' Kenneth said. 'But you from the government and all, obviously you know better…'

'No Kenneth, wait. All I mean is, you have to read things very, very carefully, to look for hidden meanings. Remember the

"Critical Reading and Scepticism" module? No? Take toothpaste.'

'You're not saying toothpaste's a cure for...'

'No I'm not. Most tubes of toothpaste say somewhere on them "no other toothpaste is better than this one." They all say it. And it's perfectly true, because all toothpastes are broadly the same, and so none of them is any better than any other one...'

'You've lost me love. What's toothpaste got to do with fish?'

'I mean, you have to read between the lines sometimes...'

'Ah I got you,' Dane said. 'I know about this.'

'Wonderful,' Mel said, relieved at any response. 'Dane, could you perhaps tell everyone what I mean? I'm sure you'll do a better job than me!'

'Yeah I read it.' Sounds of secret merriment and derision. 'I did. In the paper. It's like, say you've got the Bible or whatever, and you read it but you read it in a special way, yeah? You count all the letters or whatever. And it predicts a whole lot of things are going to happen. Like Kennedy and Princess Di and that...'

'Well that's not quite what I meant Dane...'

'So you're saying there are secret messages on toothpaste tubes?'

She felt hunted. Take a breath.

'No, Kenneth. No, I'm not saying that. All I mean is that simply because a lot of people believe something, does that make it true?'

'Well they can't all be wrong can they?'

'Why not? Why can't they all be wrong? Millions of people are completely wrong about millions of things every day.'

Uneasy shifting from June. She was thinking about it.

'Maybe the astrologers didn't get the day right after all...?'

'No no no no no. June. Look. Does it bother you at all that the whole thing is secret? Those people don't know what they're taking, do they?'

'You on the pill are you?' This was Dane, bright-eyed, fast, aggressive. Mel was reminded of what she knew about testosterone, which peaked in men at, well at about nineteen years old. Dane was seething with the stuff. Kenneth sat back and regarded him with proprietorial interest. 'You are aren't you. So what's in it?'

'Hormones.'

'What hormones? Which ones? How does it work?'

'OK, Dane. Alright. But it isn't a secret, I just don't happen to know what it is. That isn't the same thing. I could go on the internet and find out in ten minutes. All the evidence is available. Plus…'

'Yeah but…'

'Plus, it's been tested on millions of people. The doctors know it works, and they know how it works. All the experiments have been published and checked…'

'So if all those people believe it, it can't be wrong?'

Mel, unknowingly imitating Kenneth, leaned back and gave Dane a good hard looking at.

'OK Dane. The world, round or flat?' They were moving, Mel sensed, into a different phase of things here, from what the Copenhagen Protocols described as 'evaluation' to 'confrontation', and more suddenly than she had anticipated.

'You what?'

'You heard me Dane. Is the world round or is it flat?'

'Can't you look it up on the internet…?'

'I'm asking you.'

'Oh look she's off on one now…'

'I am not *off* on one,' Mel said, astonished at the swell of blood to the head, the sudden dizziness, the almost uncontrollable *emphasis* she was giving her WORDS. Do women get testosterone rushes as well, she wondered dimly? 'It's not a complicated question, Dane. The world…'

'Whatever you say it is. You're the expert. Apparently.'

'I wonder if tinned would do?' June was murmuring to a silent Kelly who was busy trying not to be noticed staring at Dane. 'If you washed the juice off first…?'

'That's a good point June,' Mel said, her voice too loud and filled with a kind of demented angry merriment. She took it down a few notches. 'Would tinned sardines do the same job as live ones? That's an interesting question isn't it? So how would you go about finding out?'

June, unhappy at being singled out in this way, looked for assistance from Kenneth, who raised eyebrows at her.

'Well you'd have to ask the priest I suppose…'

'I know, you could do an experiment couldn't you?' Mel said in her gentlest, most respectful tone. 'You could try some people on live sardines and some people on tinned sardines and see which people got over asthma the best. If anyone got over anything at all that is. Couldn't you?'

June, convinced clearly not at all by this approach, merely looked worried.

'Do you think that would be a good idea June?'

'Well as I say love, I've never actually worked with fish, not for asthma. But I'll certainly be looking into it…'

'June, if I told you that banging your head on a piece of concrete three times would cure your agoraphobia, would you do it?' Mel said, in a slightly different voice.

'Why three times?'

'How do you know it doesn't? Tried it, have you? Tested it?'

'Dane…'

'Could be the breakthrough the world's been waiting for…'

'And it'd be cheaper than all that fish…'

'Kenneth…'

'I don't like sardines…'

'Oh for Christ's *sake*…!' Mel said, aware as the sounds exited her mouth that this was not the kind of response that would be considered 'productive'. She sat back again and gathered her thoughts. Kelly glanced at her reproachfully and left. 'Sorry. Sorry everyone. So, where were we?'

'Banging our heads on pieces of concrete,' Kenneth said.

'Yes. Well, that might perhaps be a good note to finish on…'

25

Dane was ill again.

He had been up much of the night vomiting and making some fairly extraordinary noises and smells in the bathroom, hung-about closely at all times by June, hunched and cooing, with Kelly's dire presence nearby. He slept for a few hours but was awake again before dawn, clutching his stomach, calling on God. Mel, relieved that the decision had been taken out of her hands, managed to bully and manoeuvre him into her car, harassed by June right up to the motion-sensor front door and even a few desperate floodlit steps beyond it. More than once Mel found herself using the words 'statutory responsibility'. Dane writhed on the back seat, convulsed, prostrate. Mel hoped he wouldn't actually... ah. Too late. All over her ring binders. The smell bloomed up from the back, sweet and sour, tangy.

They arrived at accident and emergency no-parking-no-waiting, and Mel ushered him in. He was barely conscious. She put herself as next of kin, and sat with him for three and a half hours on a moulded plastic seat. He was asleep when they were finally called and was grouchy and uncooperative with the doctor, an exhausted chubby young man with cold damp hands.

Dane wouldn't answer questions, he just shrugged and said 'whatever'. Mel tried to fill in the details, but had no idea what Kelly might have fed him, and he wasn't saying. Had he kept any of the packaging, a nurse asked with weary patience? Yeah right, Dane offered. Was it pills, liquid, powder? Get a fucking life, Dane said helpfully.

Hours later, some unknowable time between day and night. Dane was prescribed wide-spectrum antibiotics, high dosage anti-inflammatories and some Diazepam by a busy Indian woman in blue scrubs, and discharged.

Parking had cost a fortune. Mel sat with Dane in her and Jamie's six year old Mazda. The smell inside had thickened, sweetened while they had been away, Jamie would be thrilled to discover. Brighter top notes and a new, brackish undertow. Dane nodded off again. Mel sat and considered the ticking of her indicator lamp. What she really wanted to do was take him home with her to Brittany Road, away from the source of the danger. But did she have sufficient grounds for that? He would say he'd overdone it on the lager or something, refuse a blood or urine test, Kelly would deny everything, and Mel would be left looking like a fool. She imagined the scene with her supervisor. She tried the words 'statutory responsibility' a few times, but couldn't convince herself. She sighed, and indicated left: back to Whitehawk. Dane stirred beside her.

Back at home, Mel stood over him while he took the pills, his big body shaky and hot, clammy. He was making a big deal of it.

He had no shortage of attendants; even the twins came in to solemnly look and whisper. Mel, committed as she was (of course) to the principle of non-interference with free choices made by autonomous adults, found herself almost physically guarding him from Kelly and June. Any food June brought Mel sniffed at for traces of unidentifiable matter. Paulie reappeared and made clumsy and unwelcome attempts to 'cheer him up', then fell asleep. Kenneth was nowhere to be seen.

26

And Dane perked up.

Mel had negotiated with June, agreeing to award a substantial tranche of points if Kelly could be persuaded to refrain from any further healing, for the time being. The points were worth, on current valuations, maybe thirty pounds a week. Lotsa chicken drummers, lotsa microwave garlic bread, currently a favourite of (Mel was not amazed to discover) Dane's. He would lie chewing for minutes at a time, getting butter all over the pillow cases. June was starting to run something of a tab on her future points payout. Mel was monitoring the situation. Her supervisor would no doubt have something to say about it.

Dane had decided to be grateful to Mel, and found many opportunities to express it. He would, for instance, come creeping up behind her and grab her round the neck, slobbering and nibbling the while, until she was able to wriggle free, at which he would roll his neck: "come on girl, I ain't got all day". Or he would shake her hand, but not let go, maintaining eye contact for long, long periods at a time, wrinkling his reptilian eyes, all the while doing something with his teeth and tongue, while his big ruddy body got slack and malleable.

'You did me a good turn there,' he would murmur, his hand heavy against her collar bone, spit cooling on her throat, 'no you did me a really good turn there girl. I don't forget things like that.'

June – who still, clearly, believed that he should have got a good deal worse before he started getting better – was busy with a piece of hand stitching, a martyrdom she performed on a sunlounger on the patio, in full greasy sunslap and off-white bikini. She was fine being outside, she said, as long as it was daylight and there was someone with her; that someone being (oh let's say) Dane. June had also started brazenly exposing her cleavage and substantial upper arms indoors in a sequence of citrus-coloured plunge tops, which she would, in good time, peel off to reveal the extent of the leather-like skin down her neck and over her shoulders. She wore dark glasses, indoors as well, and smoked incessantly, throatily. She and Dane baked on the scorched brick of the patio together, June frequently popping back into the cool of the kitchen to fetch drinks in big frosted glasses with a great deal of ice. Dane took care of the rolling duties, expertly, having appropriated June's sizeable stash of herbal remedy ("nice bit of gardening"), procured by Kenneth, delivered by Paulie, and, Mel was led to understand, quite reasonably priced if she fancied a bit...

In the afternoons, June slept, the midnight blue curtains slashing across the bedroom window.

Mel was suffered to join her and Dane periodically, over the next two weeks, though she noticed that June would arrange the situation in such a way that Mel was never next to Dane. Dane was to be physically available to June only. Little passed in the way of conversation on the two afternoons June spent with them, and so poor Kelly had possibly the worst imaginable audience for her rehearsals: sceptical, bored, fractious, yet tipsy enough to want to contribute to the creative discourse. Everyone knew dance. Everyone was an expert.

As for Kelly, Mel found her almost painful to watch. Her every movement was transparently directed at the single aim of getting Dane to look at her. Unfortunately, whenever (infrequently) he did offer her a glance – appraising, leering or derisive as his mood dictated – she was so overwhelmed all she could do was hide behind her unnamed friend (too shy to say), and whisper furiously.

And the routine was shaping up, Mel thought. Kind of. June had explained it to her: it was based on the themes of death and love, darkness and light, and a whole set of other binary oppositions of a subtlety and significance which was largely lost on Mel. For Kelly, however, Mel sensed that it had all become, mostly, about outfits. Kelly's dress, never exactly demure, was verging on the alarming. On this occasion she was wearing a savagely cropped string-vest halter top with appliquéd lovehearts over the nipples and the kind of shiny raspberry coloured skirt-and-pants combo favoured by ice-skaters from former Eastern Block nations. Her mate – much curvier than Kelly and lazily ogled by Dane more than once – was inclined more towards the drifty and voluminous, big baggy combats with ribbons, chiffony pastelly yokel tops, draping scarves. They both liked high strappy shoes though, and chokers. Who was death and who life, Mel was unable to say.

They were working on what Mrs. Slight called 'ensemble', synchronising their movements. There was a particular moment that was still unresolved, and which needed whole minutes of whispering and scowling. The date, Mel gathered, was approaching.

June lazily offered comments as the routine unfolded ('routine' was a word which, Kelly had confided, Mrs. Slight simply could not abide. Dance is never routine, she would say, it is transport, exaltation, transcendence. The words were huge and derisive in Kelly's small mouth, and were accompanied by expressive hand gestures. She could do it, Mel thought, but only when she didn't mean to.)

'Now this part, June drawled on into the lazy stoned July glare, as Mel settled back and Dane scrubbed violently at his chest as a hot ember fell from his smoke and singed a hair, 'this represents the death of the day and the rebirth of the night...' The two girls were huddled meaningfully, crouched on a raft of parched grass and partially-turned soil. The mate rose, jerkily, to her knees and swayed about a bit. Her arms, Mel thought, actually did look like twigs. (Assuming that that was her intention.)

'Did they make it up themselves?' Mel asked.

'No love. Well they came up with the original, what do you call it? Danie? Like in the films?'

'Concept,' Dane offered, and June slapped his calf in agreement. She was becoming quite relaxed, Mel noted. She had painted her nails.

'Concept,' June echoed. 'Well, I helped out a bit. At first they were only thinking about wearing different colours. Black and white. So I...'

'Butted in,' Dane said, and was again slapped. He rearranged his legs.

'Thank you, Mister!, no I took their idea and made up a sort of story,' she said, settling herself back, scratching her neck and absently reaching for whatever it was she didn't, at this moment, have – joint, drink, ash-tray, Dane – 'I always liked to do that when I was her age. Me and Theresa, that's my sister, we'd make up all these stories and act them out. And so I thought, you know, it could be like a battle but not a battle, more a kind of a, not a battle... Dane?'

'Dialogue.'

'Oh who's a clever boy. Dia – logue.' Her hand, randily, sought his leg and, finding nothing but slatted recliner and grease, turned the movement into a stretch. 'So yes, darkness and light, but each a part of the other, do you know what I mean love? I wished to flee, into night, to take you with me, where my heart would bid me end all deception... Course, sounds silly when you say it out like that... ' She subsided, flushed at the effort of explication, or possibly merely the effort of speaking at all, Mel wasn't certain. And what had that been in the middle? Love and deception? Big thoughts for a small hot blistered patio. Big words for a woman short of breath.

'You missed something though,' Dane said after a long meditative pause, as the girls repeatedly failed to lock fingers and make a basket of their arms, and thus represent something. 'Male and female. Isn't there any of that in here? Or is this all strictly girl on girl?' He kicked his leg back out, and this time June's purple finger nails did more than slap.

'Jesus, fuck me,' Dane said, swatting her hand away. 'Jesus, you've broken the fucking skin there girl. Fuck me!'

June lay back and, Mel was almost certain, winked at her. Almost certain.

'Also,' Dane said, stretching back but still rubbing the injured calf, and with more than a hint of that categoric thoroughness Mel had discovered in the Kui/Varney, '...also you missed youth and old age. What about youth and old age embracing? Beauty and the beast. What about that. Eh Junie?'

Mel couldn't read his tone, but June, all too obviously, could.

She strenuously did nothing for a moment, then stood and disappeared, ferociously, into the kitchen.

'What!' Dane called out, 'what did I say?' He gave Mel a complicit 'chicks' look, pulled in his belly and went after her, an unusually porky martyr. Mel could hear them, back and forth inside ('I'm not saying that am I' – 'No listen, no listen right...'), and all for a good five minutes. Mel sat on; and saw Kelly and the other girl get their clinch right for once, saw the arms go back and round, saw the friend take the fingers and twist round and back and lock, perfectly, saw it all work. They separated and stood panting like racehorses. Then Kelly glanced over – she couldn't help herself, nor could she help the grief that struck her face when she saw that Dane hadn't seen... Mel tried to do something with her face and hands that indicated that she, at least, had seen. But it was nothing, it was lost in the glare.

June and Dane came out again, from the cool kitchen.

'Kelly ate some of that what-do-you call it yesterday,' June said after a minute when she was settled again, Dane subsiding beside her; she was still flushed, Mel saw, but merry again. 'What do you call it?' June said, taking her mess of frame and needles and threads up from the baking concrete, and giving Mel low looks, 'that stuff? The green stuff?'

'Broccoli,' Mel said. Kelly eating broccoli got points.

There was quiet for half an hour, June's fingers swift and forceful with the needles, Dane stroking himself absently until he dozed off. Kelly and the friend had a ciggie break. Mel left, largely unnoticed. June rolled waterlogged eyes in her direction, and Dane offered a limp hand and a doggy leer. Kelly waved her fiercely away: one less in the garden could only mean less competition. Mel was glad to get out.

27

The Department of the Environment, Food and Rural Affairs
Date as postmark.

Dear Ms. Banff,

We are in receipt of your enquiry concerning the use of blood for ritual purposes. We assume that the blood is animal in origin: if human, then different criteria will apply.

Whilst attitudes towards the use of animal products in ritual circumstances vary both cross-culturally and also historically, the position of the present administration is best outlined in the leaflet, 'Sanguineous Ritual Practice: Know The Score!', a copy of which I am happy to enclose. (enc)

I hope this answers your questions.

Ms. K. Saloman,
Ritual Practices Team Communications Unit.

28

Sleepover. Unending heat. Much high pressure; wind, apparently, from the Azores, bringing scented breezes by day and banks of ghostly sea fog at night. Mel lay sweating in Kelly's prim pre-teen bed, listening to the sounds of the house and estate, the far away revving and shouting, the nearby slammed doors, the dogs, the brutal pumping of pulsed bass frequencies from a hundred open windows. She twisted and thumped the pillows.

Much had changed.

Paulie was back. Dane had to hand back his sofa domain, and officially left to stay with June's older sister Theresa. Or, at least, he made protracted and ostentatious farewells one afternoon, with a noisome nylon sports bag stuffed with socks and unspeakable towels, and marched up Whitehawk Way a few hundred metres, rang on the bell, and was affectionately admitted by Theresa. He was back two hours later; he just didn't have any socks any more. He seemed to be actually living in his Audi.

Kenneth was back too. He was mainly in his shed, or sitting

sweating hugely in front of UK History. Nazis and Eva Peron and Nazis again. The heat did Kenneth no favours physically: where he wasn't blotched red he was blubber white and beached and panting; he preferred to sit in the cool indoors, grotesque in tight maroon shorts, damp. He blew air out of his pursed lips and called for June. He appeared to have time on his hands.

And Boney was back.

Mel woke to him at 2.33 a.m. Kelly's room was a stuffy cabin around her, windows full open but no air, and she was sheened with sweat, she woke to a trickle into her belly button, and a finger tip lower down, inappropriately, soapily delicious...

Dane's picture scowled meaningfully at her from the wall, his hand round Kelly's shoulder, his eyes like mountains in bad weather... She lay blinking, loose, gathering herself.

Shh! She froze.

And there he went, a long slow rise – then hold – then down; raggedy, melancholy, crypted. She sat up. Quite loud, quite near, the calls. Calls? She tip-toed to the window, the nets barely stirring, the garden dim, the air thick and soupy.

There it was again, but nearer, right below, right below. She craned out of the window, it was directly underneath her head, as if she could touch it. A sudden light from downstairs; she ducked back and tried to fold the net curtain around her face as light spilled from the kitchen window onto the garden. Voices; she heard Paulie and Kenneth.

Then a terrible sound, Kelly in full throat, screaming, screaming, the man with no nose! it's the man with no nose! noooo! nooooooooo-

Cut off, as if physically muffled.

Pandemonium.

Mel grabbed for clothes, was thwarted with the legs of jeans, cursed. June shouting for Kenneth! Kenneth!

'Muuuuuum! Nooooooo. Mum don't let him…'

'It's alright love. Your mum's here love…'

Mel was down there now. June was holding Kelly, white and nervy behind the kitchen door. Kenneth and Paulie were out in the garden, shouting. Mel, feeling raw and hoaxed, shouldered her way past the sobbing women.

'Kenneth?'

'Stay away love, it's not safe right now…'

Mel, defiant, saw fit to disregard this and stood at Kenneth's shoulder, gazing out in the same direction.

'Why not? Why isn't it safe?' She tried hard not to copy Kenneth's breathy whisper.

'He's about.'

'Boney you mean?'

'Did you not hear him my love?'

'I certainly heard something, Kenneth.' She was breathing fast and hard, as Paulie went about some impenetrable business further down towards the shed, and Kenneth stood, hands on hips, looking oddly womanish.

'Kenneth, what exactly…?'

'Shh.' He raised a hand and stood motionless, eyes scanning the dark garden. 'I'm still getting something…'

'Kenneth, has anyone actually seen Boney?' Mel asked baldly, defying the implied injunction to awed silence. 'Actually?' she added.

'It's not as simple as seeing or not seeing.'

'So you haven't actually…?'

'Shh…'

Paulie was coming back up the garden now.

'That's that. I think,' he said, and dusted his hands against his trousers. He and Kenneth stood together for a moment, and then Paulie went back inside.

'I have to say, Kenneth,' Mel said, before she realised she was going to, 'that what I heard didn't really sound much like a dog. It sounded more like a person pretending to be a dog.'

'Really?' he said, very interested. 'Really? Is that what you heard?'

'I'm no dog expert, of course, but…'

'Maybe,' he said, narrowing his eyes significantly, 'what you heard didn't sound like a dog because it's a ghost. Does a ghost person sound like a live person? You've got to ask yourself.'

'Does a ghost person sound like anything at all Kenneth? Or a ghost dog for that matter?'

'I think you'll be alright now,' he said, and followed Paulie back to the house, leaving Mel feeling foolish alone in the dark. She walked down to the shed, poked about in the tall weeds behind it; she scrutinised the high fence and the gate, though what she was looking for she couldn't have said: whatever it was, there was no sign of it. Her eyes wandered to the metal shutters and graffiti next door, deserted for years. The last residents had been re-housed five years ago, no takers since then.

'Oh love?' This was Kenneth's voice again, calling from the kitchen. 'I think you might want to take a look nearer the house. Say, somewhere near the patio? Your left?'

Mel, in her own good time, found the spot; freshly turned earth, more or less directly below her window. Mel met June's dulled eyes through the kitchen doorway.

29

Thursday: discussion day. The kitchen was gleaming and smelled of Dettox and kiwi-scented washing up liquid. June was using her agenda as a fan. Mel called the meeting to order.

'I thought it might be interesting to have our debate this week about ghosts,' Mel said firmly. A stirring of dissent.

Dane said, 'Agenda says: "a debate on the question, do animals have rights?"...'

'Yes well I've changed it. The question now is: ghosts, do they exist? OK? Everyone?' Mel smiled aggressively round the kitchen table. She was aware of a buzzing sensation behind her eyes and a queasy stomach, the result of disturbed sleep and accumulated annoyance. 'Carried. Right. To kick us off, Kenneth...?'

'Do ghosts exist?' He sprawled back on his chair and folded his hands behind his head. 'Doooo...ghooo...'

'Yes, do ghosts exist? Or, another way of saying it Kenneth might be, has anyone here got any evidence – concrete, tangible evidence – that they do?' She tested each face in turn.

'Well...' June started, then fell quiet again.

'Yes June? You were about to say something?'

'Well, I was going to say that when our Theresa was living out near Gatwick she was walking down this lane one night see, dark night it was, it was completely overgrown so nobody could have…'

'June, sorry, but this is really just an anecdote isn't it?'

'A what love?'

'Anecdote. A story. What they call hearsay. It's not evidence. They wouldn't accept it in court, for instance. I'm looking for something that would stand up in court.'

'What, apart from the howling and the digging, you mean? Some kind of evidence apart from that evidence you mean?' This was Paulie.

'Anyone can howl, Paulie. Am I right?'

'You'll be telling us you can dig holes in the garden next,' Kenneth said, and Mel met his amused, malicious eye.

'Well, how difficult is that to do, Kenneth? I mean, what would you need? A spade? You could even do it with your bare hands couldn't you, the ground's soft enough. Of course you'd get soil down your nails wouldn't you?'

No response. Did Paulie slyly move his hand out of sight?

'And another question. For Paulie, this time. Paulie, what I'd like you to do is to explain how Boney, who's presumably made completely out of ghost, can dig a hole in a garden that's completely made out of soil. How does that work now? Hm? Wouldn't his little spirit paws go straight through?'

Paulie twisted his lips. 'You're asking questions no one can possibly answer…' he said, and Mel shut him off.

'OK. Kenneth. Now, every time I've heard the ghost dog noises, I've also seen either you or you and Paulie out in the back yard. At the same time. Can you explain that?'

'Look, if I'm going to get her shut up,' he indicated Kelly by a dismissive tilt of the head, 'then I've got to get him out, sharpish. What do you want me to do, sit there while she screams the bloody place down? We'd have the police out.'

'Ah. Yes. You would wouldn't you. The police. Hm. And what might they be interested in in the back yard Kenneth?'

'Don't get you love,' he said, facing her down. 'Not getting you. Not. At. All.'

'Well, I'm wondering if the police might not start to get interested in the little ghosty holes in the back? Wonder what little ghosty secrets might be buried out there? Hm?'

Halfway along the sentence she knew she'd gone too far. Kelly started to weep, with June's anxious hand soothing her. Dane stood up and, all but spitting on the floor by Mel's feet, left the room, Paulie at his heels.

'I'm still not sure I understand your question,' Kenneth said heavily, eyes locked onto her. 'Could you explain a bit about what you mean?'

Mel smiled her best smile. Like Eleni would, she thought.

'Well now Kenneth. You know me by now. We speak the same language, don't we? I only thought, where there's a mystery, there must be an explanation. And ghost dogs…'

'No?'

She shook her head.

'Uh-uh.'

The quiet sound of sobbing and consoling.

'Well. I suppose you'll have to look into it a bit more then,' Kenneth said, still leaning back at his ease, still amused. 'The hole, I mean.'

30

Mel had been summoned to see Richard, the supervisor. Well, invited anyway. Whatever. He sat across from her and smiled. Today's smell was lemon verbena. He looked like he'd had a heavy night.

'OK Mel. Now I'd like to read you the letter we received from Mr. Medcrupp and Ms Ireland yesterday, and then if you have any comments to make...'

'Sure.' She refolded her legs. The letter was handwritten on small pale blue sheets, two of them, the handwriting large and loopy. June's, she guessed.

'"Dear sir or madam, with regard to your social worker, I would like to say we are all a bit unhappy with things she has been saying. For instance, about the police. Someone should tell her she wants to keep a civil tongue in her head, we are decent people."' Fastidiously moistening a finger, he turned the page. '"And have done nothing wrong, so what's she saying that for. If you would have a word, yours faithfully, K Medcrupp and J Ireland."'

He set the letter carefully down on the low table.

'So. Mel?'

She heaved up a great sigh.

'Oh you know. Look, what I said was that maybe there was some other explanation for the holes in the back garden, maybe they should get the police in...' This, of course, was not, quite, what she'd said.

'Yes. Well somehow or other they've taken it in another way, as an accusation. Obviously we have to be extremely careful of this kind of incident.'

'Hardly an incident...'

'I know I don't need to remind you that the success of the scheme depends on goodwill and co-operation between client and...'

'Yes, I know, I'm fully aware of that.' Her tone hardened, despite her best intentions. She thought of Kelly sobbing, Kenneth's amused contempt, dismissal from Dane, June's anxious evasions. 'I've been getting lots of good will,' she said, lamely. 'Lots.'

'Heart and minds,' Richard said, and she tightly indicated her agreement.

'I'm trying,' she said.

'Your test scores have been quite remarkable, Mel. The improvements have been nothing short of extraordinary. I have the charts here, if you'd care to... You see, at the moment we have the ear of the DPM...'

'Sorry, Richard, the..?'

'Deputy Prime Minister. Both he and the Prime Minister's wife are currently taking quite an interest in our little experiment. But keeping, maintaining that interest, well that's quite another problem. Attention spans can be awfully short, as I'm sure I don't have to tell you. Funding depends on interest; interest depends on results. We need those test scores to keep coming in, Mel. We're depending on you. You're one of our Pathfinders, remember.'

'Am I?'

'Oh yes. The world, so to speak, is watching.'

'Right.'

'Any progress on finding that Master Theme?'

'Not really.' She sighed. 'I'm working on it, Richard. But it's, well you know…'

'We've all got the most tremendous confidence in you, Mel,' he said, and she considered the statement as she made her torturous, not-very-intuitive way out of the complicated building. It was perhaps, she thought, the single most disheartening thing anyone had ever said to her.

31

Inevitably, Mel found Dane and Kelly together; she wasn't even surprised, she merely nodded as she walked past the dented silver Audi one hot evening, and saw Kelly spread luxuriantly all over the back seat, Dane drooling onto and around her. Kelly, Mel presumed, had got the decoction right this time. Kelly was fully dressed, Mel noted, except that she was bare from upper midriff to mid thigh, her clothes urgently adjusted. Dane was busy, working, he had one hand down his silver and white jogging pants. Mel wasn't noticed. She walked past; she even hummed. Beware, she thought. Beware.

First thing the next morning Mel came downstairs to find Kelly hanging over Dane, her mouth to his, his hand pushed high against her breasts. They sprung apart and Mel tried to pretend not to have seen anything. But they were going to have to be more careful than this if they intended to keep it a secret, much more careful. June was everywhere. Paulie also was hanging around a fair bit.

Kelly, of course, was underage so clearly she should not have been sprawling all over the back seat of anything with anyone, let alone her cousin Dane. She should have been doing coursework for her SATs and smoking in toilets and shoplifting from Claire's Accessories. So any mention by Mel of Kelly's actual interests and activities at this point would immediately trigger some kind of official response, at the absolute (though unlikely) worst a prosecution of Dane and his redefinition as a sex offender, a paedophile. A lifetime of monitoring, intrusion and segregated Rule 45 cells. Not a great career move for him. Not a process to initiate lightly.

If Mel had believed that Kelly was in any danger from Dane then she would have started the melancholy machinery immediately by talking to Richard. But what Mel had seen as she walked past the car wasn't any sex crime, not if Kelly's face was to be believed, or the dancing that had preceded it, the eyes suddenly lit from the inside. No, whatever Dane might or might not be, and however the situation might have been brought about, there was no question in Mel's mind that Kelly was in love.

It was the hottest summer anyone could remember. Again.

32

Mel found a minute with Dane as he was getting ready to go out for the evening. He was, he said, perfectly happy to shave and talk at the same time. She stood just outside the open bathroom door, and was assailed by his shaving gel smell, carried on wafts of steam. He was engrossed in mirror and foam, and himself. Busy.

'So. Dane. June's been telling me all about you.'

'Has she now.'

'She says you're like one of the family.'

'That right?'

Mel leaned into him, into the fog of synthetic musk and citron. 'Dane, you see part of my job is to look out for Kelly. To make sure she's protected.'

'From what?'

'Anything at all that might harm her in any way. Anything, Dane.'

'You mean me?'

'I didn't say that.'

'It's not me you've got to worry about.'

'Who then?'

'That'd be telling wouldn't it?'

He stared back at her from the mirror and gave her a look that could only be interpreted one way. It involved half-closing the eyes whilst pursing the lips, and it meant come and get it. Mel remembered this particular expression from Kelly's photograph; now he was doing it to her. Despite herself, she considered him physically for a loose moment, and was surprised by the result, since ginger had never been her thing, nor tattoos and shaved heads, nor for that matter the kind of build that had an extra layer of protection under the skin. Not armoured; insulated. And then those hooded lizard eyes with the pale lashes and the casual provocation of the heavy limbs and torso, the thick neck, the slow hands... Music suddenly welling up from nowhere, singing, she could almost make out the words, was it German...? She shook herself out of it.

'Dane?' The question she wanted to ask was, have you and Kelly 'gone all the way yet?' but the form of words troubled her. She had already said the word 'protection'. Could she say 'condom'?

'Dane, Kelly's so young, she's not very experienced. What I mean is...'

'Have I porked it? No. Am I going to? Might. Any of your business? Er, no.'

Porked it.

OK, Mel thought, he's only nineteen, he's probably had a bit of a funny old start in life, all that. But 'porked it'?

'Look Dane, I have to be sure that Kelly has what we call Gillick competency, i.e. that she fully understands the implications of... You see I have statutory obligations here.'

'Like the police.'

'Bit like that, yes.'

'Weren't me guv. Wasn't even there. Know what I mean?'

'Dane, if Kelly were to... I mean, if you, and she...'

'You got a boyfriend have you?'

Mel bristled. 'Me? Yes.'

'Thought you would have, nice looking piece like you. Good job, nice money. Easy life.'

'None of this is about me…'

'You know what you're good at?'

'Why don't you tell me…'

'Asking the wrong questions.'

'So what are the right ones?'

He shrugged, shook his head.

'You don't know the half of it,' he said in much the same voice as June before him, and he was available no longer. He returned to his world of self-love and lather. He had to shave his upper arms, he said. Didn't like them bristly. Not nice for the ladies.

And I, thought Mel, watching him dripping in his scented mist of self-worship, I am getting a wee bit tired of not knowing the half of it.

July

33

The front room of number 23 was thick and airless with heat. Mel was waiting for Kenneth to finish a spatial logic test. They were both sitting in front of the television, upon which terrible lunatics were pursuing their various insane grievances by the use of threat, sarcasm and common assault. Kenneth said he preferred to have a bit of noise on while he worked, but Mel couldn't see how it was helping. Was he sure he wouldn't prefer to watch one of the videos on her list? Perhaps 'Seeing The Other Side,' the one where two warring neighbours find common ground and a healthy mutual respect through a shared involvement in a community…

'Love. Eastenders is on.'

Kenneth became thoughtful half way through the test, and Mel watched optimistically. The screen was full of bulging neck veins and the raw red mouths of screaming women, and by the speed of the cross-cutting it was clear they were all heading straight for a good therapeutic blood-letting any minute.

'Can I ask you something?' he said, and she said yes, of course, anything you like. These were good signs, she thought.

'Something about the test?'

'No something about Dane. Is he shafting our Kelly?'

Mel tried hard not to react, but feared her face had betrayed her. She reached for the remote and lowered the sound. The demented faces screamed silently behind her.

'Kenneth. You know I'm not allowed to discuss anything like that. That would come under "confidentiality"...'

'I'll take that as a "yes" then.'

'Have you got any reason to think that might be happening?'

'Paulie. He thought he heard them at it the other night. I've seen her looking at him all day. I've seen her skipping out the bathroom with hardly a stitch on while he's outside. Hanging round the couch.' He fluttered his hands. 'See, she don't understand about boys, and Dane's such a fucker. He's just a big cock with this stupid little fucker attached to it.'

'Have you spoken to her about it?'

'No, I wanted to get my evidence straight first. Like you say.' He was fiddling with his phone now. 'Yeah. Paulie mate? Yeah it's go. Yeah today. Yeah, now.'

'Kenneth?'

'Making arrangements love. Nothing for you to worry about.'

He went back to the test, the pen scratching deeply and viciously as it ticked multiple-choice boxes. He was getting everything right, she noted. She suspected that Dane might have been coaching them all, since scores had been suddenly and – all professional modesty aside – inexplicably moving upwards since his arrival. Every batch she sent off to the RU was better than the last. It was all a bit too good to be true, she thought. Someone got thrown into a canal on the television.

An hour later, she was packing up to leave for the day when Dane came banging in through the kitchen door from the back garden. He was bent over, holding his leg, high up, near the crotch. There was blood, it was trickling over his hand and onto June's spotless white rug.

'Mel? Fuck's sake, get me out of here will you...'

34

'Same shit different sofa' might have been Dane's T-shirt slogan. He collapsed onto Mel's plum three-seater and was immediately in total and unarguable possession. Things gathered around it, as if by some power of calling he possessed. Kelly had clearly been dispensing again before he left, and Dane was sick. Mel put the plastic mop bucket beside him, just in case. Jamie, happily, was out, so she could settle him without any flak. Jamie, she sensed, was going to get on with Dane like a house that is not on fire. After Jamie, she would have to explain it to June, Kelly, her supervisor, the Rationality Unit switchboard. She sat staring blankly at Dane. His mobile went off a couple of times, as did her own: she ignored both of them.

'Hello June? It's Mel here.'
'Oh love we've been that worried…' June's voice was thin and needly down the phone.
'Nothing to worry about June,' Mel said crisply, irritated at once by June's apocalyptic tone. 'Everything's fine. Dane's with me now and he's right as rain, nothing serious, he just needs to sleep.'

'Oh love.' For a moment June was overwhelmed and Mel picked at a finger nail impatiently at the sounds. 'OK. So we'll see you in a while then will we? What time is it now… Kenneth, it's Mel, she says he's alright.' Mel could hear murmuring and sleepy movement as Kenneth stirred, said he could have told her that, rolled over again.

'June? Now there's absolutely no problem at all. But Dane's a bit groggy right now, so I thought it would be best if he came here, to Brittany Road.'

'Brittany…?'

'My place June. The place where I live.'

'I'm not… hold on a minute love, let me get… no Kenneth she says he's at her place. No Dane is.'

'June?'

'Whatever is he doing there?'

Mel felt the need to assert control against June's almost limitless wooliness. 'June, listen for a moment. Dane's with me here. I think that's best for now.'

'Let me talk to him. Put him on. No Kenneth they're not in the hospital anymore…'

'Well he's asleep June,' Mel said, watching Dane stir luxuriously. 'The doctor said he should sleep it off.'

The door slammed downstairs: Jamie. She made a quick panicked survey of the room, tried somehow to minimise the great mass of Dane who seemed suddenly to fill the whole room, the whole world. She all but hung up on June and sat stiffly waiting for Jamie's key in the lock.

'Mel? What's that stink?'

35

Mel had no qualms about trying to use Dane's dependent condition to her own advantage: she saw it, in fact, as a heaven-sent opportunity. The Copenhagen Protocols emphasised the need to 'exploit moments of transition', and Mel was, for once, in full agreement.

'Dane, look, tell me what's going on here,' she said point blank at him, as he lay prostrate on the sofa. He stared her down. Clearly, he felt no moment of transition to be occurring. Leer.

'Why should I?'

Mel hesitated. But not for long.

'Dane, now you know how important client confidentiality is to me...'

'Yeeees...'

'And you remember how we all signed agreements about it?'

'So?'

'But sometimes there can be reasons – good reasons, Dane – for breaking it. Now for instance, if child protection issues were to come up... I mean, purely as an example, it might be necessary on child protection grounds for me to tell Kenneth that I have concerns about Kelly. And you. Together. I might even have to tell Kenneth exactly where you're holed up. What Kenneth does with that information is, of course, outside of my control…'

'You threatening me?'

'I'm presenting possible future scenarios, Dane. I'm presenting you with some of the possible consequences of your actions. You remember we talked about taking responsibility for your…'

'Think I'm scared of old fatty Ken?'

'Oh yes, I think so. I think he's got something on you already. I don't think he'd be all that pleased to hear anything about you and, for instance…'

'Look don't go on about it alright? Fuck me, girl.'

Mel sat back and pondered him.

'I ask questions, you give answers OK?' she said.

'Shoot'

What to ask first, she thought?

'Who injured you? Kenneth?'

'With his bad back? You're joking aren't you?'

'Why are the twins like this?'

'Cos I told them about these Muslims I saw on the telly. All covered up and not allowed to say anything. Just the women had it.'

'Right,' Mel said, feeling none the wiser. 'And why did you tell them that?'

'To shut them up. They were going on. So I said, they should be like these Muslims and not ever say nothing and be covered up all the time. I told them they could take it in turns. They'd get martyred by stoning if they didn't.'

'Martyred. Right.'

'So they take it in turns now. One of them's the woman, and the other one's the priest, then they swap next day.'

'Yes but... shut them up? About what?'

'This and that. The other. That kind of thing. Obviously I never thought they'd take it on full time did I? I just thought they'd like the dressing up. Some religions are like that though. Dead sticky.'

'Sticky... Dane, do you know anything at all about religion...?'

'Yeah, told you already, saw it on the telly in clinky.'

'And you don't think it's possible there's a little bit more to it than that? No? OK.' She plucked a strand from the air. 'The wedding dress. Kenneth was shifty about it.'

'Oh yeah, was he?' Dane shifted, shiftily. She pressed on.

'And why Marke? Why the final e?'

'You what?'

'Kenneth's kingly name. It's got a final e.'

'Yeah? Beats the shit out of me, Sherlock.'

'Alright then. Boney.'

'Boney?' Dane crossed his legs, the duvet shifting and folding around him. 'What about him?'

'Have you seen him?'

Dane gave her his 'get a life' face. 'Yeah right. Fucking doggy-woggy from beyond the grave. Scooby-dooo. Woof.'

'OK then.' Her tone was getting grimmer. 'Why does Kelly dance when it's perfectly obvious to anyone that she...'

'Steady now...'

'...is finding the discipline a considerable challenge...?'

'One way of putting it I suppose. Me, I'd have said she looks like a camel in drag getting 20,000 volts up its arse.'

Mel raised eyebrows at the paraphrase. 'So why then? She doesn't even seem to enjoy it. Mrs. Slight said that it was Kenneth who wanted her to do it. And...' This was trickier. 'Dane? I know it isn't really any of my business, but what brings

173

you here all of a sudden? June thought you weren't coming.'

'Fancied a holiday by the seaside didn't I.' Weren't me guv/wasn't there was I/ don't know what you're going on about do I? Delete as appropriate. She remembered Dane's alarmingly high aggregate rationality index. Clever enough to know how to hide it.

'Dane, when we spoke before, you said it wasn't you I should be worried about. About Kelly I mean.'

'Uhuh.'

'What did you mean? Who should I be worried about then?'

'If I were you, lover,' he said, closing his face right down and managing to convey menace solely by leaning back and breathing differently, 'I'd worry about you.'

Jamie, obviously, wasn't about to leave Mel alone on the premises with some ginger hooligan. His method of protecting her was to smoke a vast quantity of cannabis and pass out in the bedroom, cunningly remaining fully dressed, in case of emergency. Mel lay awake beside him and heard Dane's small sounds from next door, rustling, scratching, the occasional mighty sinus-clearing snort. His mobile went off every thirty minutes or so, vibrate then ring. Text received. She heard the muted beeps as he texted back.

And what, she thought dimly as Jamie drooled and snorted beside her, was she going to do now? Was there an appendix in Operations /Protocols /Methodologies to cover this? She thought of the horrible shiny ring binders, now splattered with Dane's sick; she'd tried to clean them off but they were getting less and less attractive with every passing day. They were now shoved in a plastic bag at the bottom of the wardrobe. What would she look it up under anyway? Ginger hooligans (or was it more like brass?) Her thoughts fled about her, like mice. She crept out to the kitchen and rang the Rationality Unit switchboard, which was, of course, closed. The recorded voice faded and broke up a couple of times, all Mel could make out was "... or contact your line manager, Practice Manager or other first-line..." She left a whispered message, detailing the facts so far and her decision to remove Dane from the situation, then slipped back to bed and was gradually immured in uneasy dreams of exposure and escape.

'Who's there?'

She woke to someone in the room, her bedroom. She struggled clear of the comatose Jamie and found the light switch. Time?, she demanded groggily. Hello?

'Dane?'

He was standing by the window, naked, staring out. She felt a sudden rush of fear of him. She slid out of bed and reached the door. Jamie stirred quietly.

'Dane?' She tried to whisper, but he was oblivious to her. She couldn't be sure that he wasn't sleepwalking. 'Dane? Shouldn't you go back to bed?'

'Who is calling me?' he said, and Mel felt a shudder of weirdness come over her at the sound.

'Dane, are you OK?' she said, as normally as she could manage.

'Where have I been? Where am I?'

'You're at Brittany Road. Remember?'

'What did I hear?'

'What did you... Dane, you're not really awake properly are you?' she said cautiously.

'Is that what you think?' His voice was smoke and fallen leaves, deeply submerged. His gaze was miles away. 'I know differently but I am not able to tell you. Where I awoke, there I was not, but where I was I cannot tell you. I did not see the sun, nor did I see land and people: but what I did see…'

'…you cannot tell me, probably. Right. Right. OK.'

She approached him with tiny steps, reached out a hand and touched his thickly muscled shoulder; no response. His eyes were open but fixed, staring out at the house over the road. Dane, she realised, was pulling gently, absently, at his foreskin, rolling the tip between thumb and forefinger, a joint burning between his fingers, while his gaze wandered away, to the east, to Whitehawk. The sky was starting to lighten, the roofs and parked cars solidifying into patches of grey, ash, dove, slate. A bright red recycling box on a doorstep started to glow the colour of dried blood. Seagulls wheeled and screamed overhead, an early-bird's car door slammed nearby. Dane's voice crept out again:

'The crash that I heard behind me

Was death's door closing.

The light – when will it be extinguished?

When will Night come to the house?'

'Death's door,' Mel said. 'Uhuh. Right. Er Dane, now do you think we can maybe get you back into bed?' she said, and patted – so gently – his freckled shoulder. She was horribly aware of his nakedness, and unwilling because of it to attempt any further contact. She did, however, manage to take the joint from his fingers. 'How about it Dane? What do you say? Hm?' A car was failing to start outside, coughing and grinding, and it sounded familiar. Mel wondered for a moment who it might be at this hour of the day; early shift on the loony ward for Martha over the road perhaps? Mel tried to make her voice quietly persuasive, but wasn't certain she was hitting the right tone. She was abruptly sure that Dane was in some drugged, hallucinated state, and that Kelly had a hand in it. 'Dane, did you take anything that Kelly gave you?'

Slow nodding, as if to some other question entirely.

'Then was the most searing
Magic unleashed…'

'Right. Right.' She held his arm and attempted to guide him away from the window and back to the front room couch. He was, she knew, hugely strong under his layer of insulation: only a day or two ago she had seen him pick June up in one arm and lift her clear off the ground. He was hot and clammy to the touch, the thick pelt glistening, thighs slick with sweat.

He settled back onto the sofa with a sigh, twitching the tangled duvet over his lower legs, and she watched him as he slept again, his open mouth drooling peacefully onto her expensive jade velvet cushions, liquid phrases slipping from his tongue in what sounded now like German. She sat in the other chair and allowed her eyes to droop. She had a Practice Meeting at 10.30, she had a report to finish before that, it was now – what? – 6.00am. The Rationality Unit would open at 9.00, she would need to talk to them right away. It'd been a long night. She fetched the alarm clock from the bedroom and set it for 7.30. Jamie slept on. She pondered him briefly: she couldn't remember what time he needed to be up today. He'd have to manage himself. She settled drowsily in the armchair and tried to remember when she'd last eaten anything. There was, she knew, nothing except a bag of deliquescent salad leaves and some slightly crusty guacamole in the fridge. She could have done with some of June's chicken nuggets, she thought, and sighed heavily, as Dane stirred and murmured. A soothing sort of a sound. Seagulls had nested on one of the chimneys nearby and the dumpy baby seagull cried all night for fiiiiish, his frantic scratchy little voice coming sometimes for hours at a time. Mel had on more than one occasion considered chucking a tin of tuna at him herself. Soothing though, like distant singing; all the longing in the world…

She shook herself awake. Files, she was thinking. Files.

She found them in a nasty heap underneath a pile of newspapers waiting to be recycled by the front door.

Innumerable highly skilled professionals – all empathetic, intuitive individuals, and acutely sensitive to the various psycho-socio-emotional-economic eddies and currents swirling around him – had laboured diligently and long to assess, analyse, describe, investigate, catalogue and tabulate the entity that was Kenneth Medcrupp over the last fifteen years. His file was gravid with insight and tentative prognosis. Wry notes of guarded scepticism occasionally surfaced; one community mental health nurse, for instance, had issued a report which ended with the statement: 'Kenneth Medcrupp exhibits an admixture of guileless eccentricity and something altogether more calculated.' A police community liaison officer noted Kenneth's 'absolutely untrustworthy manner'. But overall the verdict was that Kenneth was feckless and deluded but represented no threat. Nothing very recent though, Mel thought, flipping the pages. And it was all so boring…

Awake again, no idea what time now, Dane was standing over her again, for a moment she thought he must have been in the shower, but he was simply running with sweat. He was still naked, except for the bandage round his thigh. His smell was staggeringly strong. He was speaking animatedly, pushing his mobile phone into her hand. He retreated from her.

'Dane…?'

'Shhhhh.' The front room was as dim and cool as a church hall. 'Shhhh,' he said again, and lay back on the sofa. 'I'll say it and you text it. Fingers too slippy. You text it. OK?'

'Dane…'

'Shhhhhhh. This fearful longing/that sears me/this languishing flame…'

'Woh. Slow now…'

'…what strokes of death could ever make it yield…'

'What?'

'Text it.'

Mel fiddled with the tiny buttons. The phone was wet, presumably from contact with Dane's body.

wt strks/dth cld evR m8k i yield? she typed, and felt idiotic.

'Dane, really…'

'Send.'

'Who to?'

'Kelly. Send it to Kelly.'

'Will she be awake now do you think Dane…?'

'Send it to Kelly.'

Mel complied.

'Is she coming?' he said. 'Can you see her coming? The ship, can't you see it yet?'

'Ship?'

'Ship. Shhhhhhhh.' He drifted off again, absently handling himself. Mel relaxed.

Too soon, he was up and shouting again, dragging the duvet around him.

'Bring her. Bring her. Bring her…'

'Dane…'

'Shhh. Bring her. Shhhh.' He was holding his hand to her

mouth to quiet her, he was pulling her arms and hands, up, up!

'Bring her! Bliss beyond bounds, joyful delirium…'

'Sorry Dane, that's my phone. Hello?'

Kelly's voice on the other end, fiercely whispering.

'You've got to stop them. Now. Now!'

'Kelly?' The line went dead. 'Kelly? Where are you?'

Mel grabbed her car keys and fled.

'And you,' she yelled back at Dane, 'you stay here until you hear from me. Understand?'

The Health and Safety Executive
An Agency of the Home Office
Date as postmark

Dear Ms. Banff,

With reference to your enquiry concerning the setting of bonfires on private land, I am happy to enclose a leaflet, 'Playing With Fire!', which contains recommendations and answers to frequently asked questions (minimum safe distance from dwelling, etc), as well as useful telephone numbers and a checklist.

I hope this answers your query satisfactorily,
Yours sincerely,

Mr. V. Pinsent,
Domestic Land Use Team Communications Desk.
(enc: HSE 2825, rev.)

The house was dark and silent as Mel pulled up. She shut the car door as quietly as the mechanism allowed and scooted round the side, down the passage to the back garden, unseen.

'Kelly?' she hissed into the darkness. There was no sign of her. In fact there was no sign of anyone. Mel stood looking up at the back, feeling oddly dumbfounded. She felt herself watched, and made a show of walking straight to the back door. She knocked, lightly, on the glass panel.

'Hello? June?'

She peered through the glass. The kitchen was a dim blur. She ducked back away from the door into the garden. 'Hello? Anyone?' She briefly considered howling like a dog to see if that would get any action, but quickly decided against it.

The back door was locked. The key, she knew, was located under the third plant pot along on the kitchen windowsill, a low struggling herb of some kind. She located the key, cold and slippery in her hot fingers. She smelled a waft from the plant, like old coins on the tongue. Her fingers were smeared with some kind of slime, and she wiped them against her jacket. The smell was familiar.

The key was difficult in the door, she wrestled with it for a few anxious moments. 'I had reasonable cause to attempt to enter the property,' she heard herself thinking loudly, 'because I had reason, good reason, to believe that the welfare of a minor was at stake.' The lock wasn't yielding.

'Or you could call it breaking and entering', she thought.

She stood back gave the glass panel a good kick. The noise was for a moment bewildering. She imagined track-suited hordes gathering from the many hidden corners of Whitehawk, rising up in a miasma of shaving-gel and wet dog to accuse her. She stood, panting, listening: nothing. She kicked out some shards of glass from the door and snaked her hand up and found the catch. The door swung satisfyingly open. She was, so far, impressing herself with her proficiency.

The kitchen was scrubbed and glinting in the dim light from the garden. Mel hesitated to go further into the house, although she felt certain her noisy destruction of the back door must have raised anyone within. She was surely alone here. So where was Kelly? The call had been from a mobile; thus it, and she, could be precisely anywhere, Mel thought, cursing herself for not thinking it sooner.

Her eye was caught by an unfamiliar look to the front room/dining room, which opened directly off the kitchen. Mel peered round in, and for a moment couldn't understand how it could possibly be the same room.

The whole of the centre was now taken up with trestles which were covered, so far as Mel could make out, with cling-film-covered dishes and bowls and trays. The sofas, television, side cabinets, coffee tables, all had been moved away somewhere. The room was dressed for a party. She noted glints from ranked bottles and stacked cases of beer in the corner. Frosted balloons shifted overhead tethered by thin shiny ribbons, answered by paper plates and plastic glasses, all with co-ordinating designs of flying champagne corks. Could you get all this at Lidl? Mel found herself wondering. Or had Kenneth had to pay a visit to a cash and carry?

She reached the head of the stairs, and found herself crouched and sweating and hardly daring to breathe.

'OK,' she said out loud, and stood straight and took a proper breath. 'Fuck this.' Either I'm alone here or I'm not. But I'm no burglar.

'Hello?' she called up the stairs, twisting her face into a suitably interrogative posture. 'Hello? June? Kenneth? It's Mel.'

Nothing back.

She found the light switches for the ground floor and flicked them on. The scale of the transformation was immediately apparent; the whole ground floor was themed now, with shiny plastic ivory and cartoon champagne corks everywhere. Banners stretched out, from one side to the other: Congratulations! Musical notes, exclamation marks.

Mel stood at the foot of the stairs and considered. She had to find Kelly. That was obviously her first priority. But Kelly, clearly, wasn't here. So what exactly was her business in this house, at this time? She imagined the cross-examination: so, you might say you were acting on a 'hunch' at this moment Ms. Banff? Nasty, sneering delivery on 'hunch.' Innocent, muttered Mel to herself, and began to ascend the stairs. Innocent, your honour. Welfare of a minor. Children's Act. Sufficient grounds. All that. She'd have been happier if her supervisor had known, though, but it was too late for that now. And she had at least partially covered her back by leaving a message on the Rationality Unit switchboard about Dane, although she couldn't be certain exactly how clear she'd been.

Kelly's room. Again the change was complete. No gingham check, no boybands, and, most strikingly of all, no pictures of

Dane anywhere to be seen. There were little bald patches in the paintwork where the sticky pads had been removed, and none too carefully by the look of it. The room was stripped down and was now no more than a small, impersonal guest bedroom. Mel stood and attempted to make sense of it, but nothing led anywhere, certainly not in the direction of Kelly.

Sure though she now was that the house was empty, she still couldn't open the door to June and Kenneth's room without some hesitation. She had never set foot in here, had never been invited to, and in fact had never included the room in her internal map of the house. What conceivable business could she have in here?

She flicked on the light. The first thing that took her eye was a dress, laid out on the double bed. It was a large cream and white number, three-quarter length sleeves, and not very much in the way of shape. Perfect for a somewhat overweight middle-aged woman, Mel thought. She shut the door and another dress was hanging on the back, this one little more than shreds and scraps artfully stitched together over an elasticated body, resulting in a kind of Disney-fied elfin quality. A dance costume, Mel felt sure. What was it June had said about the theme of Kelly's performance? The dress probably represented it in some esoteric way that Mel couldn't see. Behind it was another one, similar but in contrasting colours and slightly smaller, presumably for the unnamed friend. Light and darkness/love and death? Something like that.

Mel was halfway back down the stairs when she caught movement in the back garden through the landing window. She ducked back against the wall, then craned forward to peer out. There was no moon but she could just about make out a tiny shape clambering over the fence from next door, closely followed by another.

She took the stairs two at a time and wrenched the back door open. Light flooded the garden in a steep triangle.

'Michael? David? What are you doing out so late? What are you carrying?' They tried to run for it but Mel was strong and fast, and held one in each hand.

'Michael, what have you got here…?' She shook him and the bundle of clothes rolled away from his grasp and fell to the grass. Mel was struck immediately by the fact that that these weren't just any clothes: these were girls' clothes.

She smiled unconditionally up at the faces hanging anxiously in front of her.

'Fellas? Shall we have that talk now?'

The twins were no easy nut to crack, having been soundly terrified by Dane concerning what would happen to them if they were to go blabbing. He'd even given them a Koran, which one of them was carrying. Allah, Dane had told them, hates a grass worse than poison. A grass is the one thing gets right up Allah's nose. He don't never forgive it, and when you die you know what he does? He gets a big dagger right, just like Kenneth's, and he heats it up right, and he sticks it…

'I see.'

'So he said the way to stop it happening was to have rule of silence. That way, one person would be the woman so she couldn't speak, and the other one would be the priest, to make sure she didn't. And if she did then the other one could throw stones at her.'

'And you swap over every day?'

Solemn nodding.

'And the clothes?' Well, she thought, it was obvious really. If they were going to take it in turns to be the woman, they'd need a supply of women's clothes, girls' clothes, from washing lines.

For underneath the duvet cover. Stands to reason. Identical eight-year-old cross-dressing Islamists on a panty raid, she thought faintly. I mean, why not?

'Oh yeah? Well I read the Koran as well,' she said, and the twins stared up at her with their moon faces. 'Of course I do! Let me see it for a minute, there's a bit somewhere...' Michael handed over the book and Mel riffled the pages. Where reason had failed, let authority prevail. Odd phrases caught her eye, it all seemed to be about darkness and light. Allah took away their light and left them in utter darkness... He brings them out of darkness into the light... 'Ah here we are,' she said, and raised her eyebrows in a suitably grand manner:

'"And another thing I say unto you that gets right up my nose is children who keep secrets from... you know, people... I hate that even worse than being a grass, actually, come to think about it."' She slammed the book shut again quickly. 'Did you never see that bit?'

They shook their heads.

'No? Well that's what it says. Right here.' She handed it back to Michael. 'So maybe it might be better if you tell me what I want to know? Maybe? In terms of, you know, the afterlife...'

Michael folded his arms across his chest and tried to be all sceptical, but was nudged by the shrouded other and gave a reluctant gesture of acquiescence. Fear of Dane was balanced on a knife edge with fear of red hot daggers, and daggers were gaining rapidly. The garden was emerging from the darkness, the shed at the far end a deep enveloping shadow, the house a blank grey edifice. Mel improvised a gesture, hands piously together and eyes rolled up to, approximately, heaven, where Allah was deep in sombre judgement of the situation. The twins checked with each other.

OK.

'So, what is it Dane says you're not supposed to tell anyone about?'

David grinned helplessly at Michael.

'I mean, is it something someone said? Or something you've seen…'

Seen. Clearly.

'What, out here in the back garden?' Slow nodding. 'At night? When you're out finding clothes? And what was it?'

They'd clammed up again; Mel shook her head, no, it was the red hot burning dagger up the arse for these two, her face said, and the twins gave up the struggle.

'Well one time we was out the back and we saw dad.'

'Kenneth?'

'Yeah, and Uncle Paulie.'

'And what were they doing sweetheart?'

Giggling.

'They were having a game.'

'What in the middle of the night? In the back garden?'

'Yeah. They were playing doggies.' More giggling. 'They were being silly.'

'How do you play doggies? What do you do? Can you show me?'

Much reluctance. David got down on his knees and made scrabbling gestures in the grass.

'You dig?'

'Yeah to hide things in. And then you go like this…' A strange sound came from his mouth. The other one did it as well, the garden was full of their unearthly wailing.

'OK OK. Shhhh,' she said. 'But why? What does your dad and Uncle Paulie hide in the hole?'

Giggling. Michael raised his hand to his nose.

'I don't get you…' she said.

Then she did: if you had to hide a body part, where would you put it? Kenneth's question in the Mentorn Hotel family network group conference. What was hidden in the back garden was a nose. Gary Chope's, to be precise. Kept as a trophy from the incident with Dane. Kept hidden in the back garden, and brought out for – well, Mel couldn't imagine quite what purpose Kenneth might have with a severed human nose. But this was, she thought, starting to make sense.

'And so your dad and Uncle Paulie, they dig up the nose and then pretend it was a dog that dug the hole? Like a game?'

Slow serious nodding.

'Fellas, look, this is really important, do you know where Kelly is? Right now I mean? It wouldn't be telling tales to tell me. In fact…'

She realised she had lost the twins' attention, their eyes had wandered to the back of the garden, where the cement shed was looming into view. The flaking green door was opening. Mel peered into the gloom.

Kenneth.

38

Kenneth's shed was big enough to allow two comfortable chairs and a huge old Bang and Olufsen television with teak pretensions. It was, Mel thought, more what an American might call a den than a shed. Apart from a single spade there were no rusty garden implements, no lawn mower, no heaps of broken timbers or tubs of creosote. Nothing but bags of cement stacked up in one corner, the spade, a hoary old leather case, and a pervasive smell of old burn and damp carpet. The one window, covered with thick plastic, was further obscured on the outside by brambles.

Kenneth sat in the scruffier of the two chairs, legs sprawled out in front of him, black socks and white trainers, fat pink calves, pudding knees. He was playing with the masterfully understated remote control, balancing it on one finger and rotating it until it became unstable and started to fall. The sword of kingship was by his feet, lying on a piece of velvet.

'I been in here all night,' Kenneth said dreamily. 'Looking at some old videos. Want to see?'

Mel, uncertain of his mood, sat in the other chair. Kenneth pushed 'play.' He had the sound on mute.

It was a sequence of clips of home movies. Christmas trees and birthday cakes, children grimly playing recorders, comedy with fat four year olds in tutus doing dumpy pirouettes. Mel didn't at first recognise Kelly, aged three, aged five. She was a chubby shy creature, dimple cheeks and an obedient but reserved smile. In one clip she could be seen running from the camera on a stretch of glittering autumn grass, flinging herself into the air, twisting and turning. The camera turned back on itself and there was a younger, thinner Kenneth, the cameraman, pulling a zany face.

'Most of her dance stuff's on separate tapes. This is all holidays and that.'

The quality of the picture suddenly improved, the colour became more solid, the tracking smoother. New technology. Kelly was now perhaps eight. The camera panned over a soggy windswept field, dotted with tents, one of which had collapsed and was flapping in a hopeless delinquent heap. Rain got onto the lens, and the picture abruptly stopped.

'Cornwall,' Kenneth said, shortly. 'We go every year to see my brother Malcolm. Every fucking year it rains. Course she won't do it now. Thinks camping's beneath her.'

Another year. Kelly, aged ten, dressed in what June would undoubtedly call 'the wrong clothes for camping', a thin pink strappy top and cut offs: she was huddling against the wind on a rock surrounded by gorse. And where, Mel wondered, was June in all this?

Sudden flash of overexposure and glare. Abroad now. Spain, Mel wondered?

And here was June, she was sitting on a bed in a hotel room, unpacking and swatting at the cameraman. A view from a balcony, a brilliant azure pool, new built and pristine. A group shot, with the camera presumably resting on something: Kenneth, Kelly (maybe 12?), June – and Dane.

'Twins went to stay with Theresa, June's sister, so we had a break from them. They had to get special Christmas presents to make up for it. Never heard the last of it.'

Frolics in the mosaic-ed pool. June screaming and wading away from someone: it's Dane. He lunges underwater and then June disappears, legs first, in an explosion of spray. The next shot is unclear, taken from too close: the camera backs away slowly, until June's more-than-generous cleavage comes into focus, her chicken-skin folds and blue thread veins filling the screen. Her dripping bikini top is not, perhaps, quite big enough for its job. Another fuzzy close up, the picture dark until Mel was able to make out bristly golden hair, a thigh, and a familiar pair of over-stuffed black Speedos. Also wet. Dane. She almost blushed. And why was there now no footage of Kenneth and Kelly, she thought?

'You see,' Kenneth said into the silence, 'my duty is to my office. My blood. To continue the line until exile ends.'

'Kenneth, I don't think I understand what you're saying to me,' Mel said, aware of a creeping weirdness in the air.

'Kingship has burdens as well as rights. I have a dynastic duty to marry.'

'And what does June think about that?'

'June and I have an agreement. We always have had. June is the mother of David and Michael. Michael is the older by ten minutes, so he will inherit. Tough on David of course, but there it is, it's primogeniture, it's the way things are.'

'Kenneth, I got a phone call from Kelly about half an hour ago. She sounded frantic. Do you know what that might be about? Do you know where she is now?'

Ken shrugged. His eyes didn't leave the television screen.

'I had quite an interesting chat with the twins a few moments ago Kenneth.'

'Yeah. I heard.' As he had, presumably, heard the noises of her destruction of the back door.

'Tell me if I've got this all wrong,' Mel said. 'Last summer you and Kelly's father, Gary Chope, had, what? a disagreement? About Kelly?'

'Could call it that.'

'It turned into a fight. Here. In the back garden.'

'Gary, he come back here last year, messing round Kelly, sniffing round, threatening me, he got what was coming to him. Dane saw to that.'

'Dane cut his nose off.' Gary Chope, medicated and rocking in a psychiatric day unit, head down, face hidden in his invariable white scarf. The Man With No Nose. Kelly's dad.

'You buried it in the garden, you kept it. Boney was Gary's dog. You hacked his head off. You buried him out here. Gary escaped and went to the police.'

'Well that's what happens when you go sniffing round where you're not wanted. Know what I mean?' (Mel duly noted the threat.) 'And silly bugger, but didn't our Daney go and leave a whole lot of blood on the dagger. Cut himself didn't he, well what do you expect from a dickbrain like that, but blood everywhere… Dear oh dear. So if police ever did get interested again – and I'm not saying they would – then that's physical evidence, what you might call forensic evidence. And I know how important evidence is to you love, we'll be getting round to that in a minute… But you can't argue with DNA. Now can you?'

'You kept the nose as part of the evidence against Dane. You're blackmailing him about it. You didn't want me to touch the dagger. Because I wasn't in the blood line…'

'You'd have mixed up the DNA. Can't have that. So anyway, our Dane, yeah he pretty much does what I tell him. I say jump, he says how high.'

'Go on.'

'See, to start with you were mostly a problem of management. You might have noticed that you weren't always one hundred percent welcome, not in all circles, not at all times? Did you ever notice that at all?' He was leaning, mocking; she wanted to smack him a good one. She made herself look calm and professional.

He cosied in.

'You see, June has never been what you might call a wife to me. Not really. June, she doesn't really understand the obligations of kingship. And of course she's not going to be producing any more heirs now is she? Overweight, over-age, I'm not exactly going to go poking around in that old mess now am I? Dear me no. And then, what if something were to happen to Michael or David? I'm not saying it would. But I have to think about these things.' His voice was a self-satisfied purr.

'So it's not June that you're marrying?'

Another clip: Kenneth in a thick brown corduroy coat and woolly cap, Kelly, about her real age, in gangster drag, charcoal suit and pencilled moustache, complete with cheroot and trilby, which is far too big for her. She is leaning against Kenneth in a way that Mrs. Slight would describe as 'in character', her face a mask of knowingness and allure.

'June? No love. Not Junie. Not as it happens no.'

Something inside Mel lurched and was seasick as she saw Kelly reach up and give Kenneth a lipsticky kiss. He was hunched low to receive it, but even so managed to turn his face to the camera and wink. The kiss was surprisingly long.

'It's Kelly isn't it.'

Not a question; it was suddenly obvious. Kenneth stretched out a foot and worried at an edge of carpet.

'Kelly is promised to me. June and me worked it out years ago. Dane, he betrayed me. His own flesh and blood. Paulie didn't finish him off but I will. He's going for a long drive in the country. He isn't having her.'

'Kenneth, I surely don't have to remind you that no one's supposed to be "having her" at all, least of all... She's fourteen years old.'

No answer and Mel was certain that Kenneth was trying not to say something. His face was twisted into an expression of such revolting smugness that Mel could almost hear his thoughts. What he was doing, she realised, was trying not to boast.

'Isn't she?'

Raised eyebrows.

'No actually love Kelly Ireland will be twelve years old in nine days time.'

Mel stood, she was leaving already, she was looking for Kelly.

'Kenneth, you know full well that nothing like that can possibly happen. I'll have her on the at-risk register so fast you won't know...'

'No you're not in such a hurry are you love?' Kenneth lazily stood and took another video out, ejected and inserted, all very clattery. He slumped back again with a 'whoof.'

'One more.'

Mel, still standing by the door of the shed, watched the shaky grainy picture form and saw something that brought all the blood in her body to a terrible sudden stop. She saw her house in Brittany Road, dark, her bedroom window lit against the shadows, a heavily-built naked man taking up much of the light: Dane. He is saying something, looking behind him, into the room, playing with his foreskin. A shadow appears at his back, a hand reaches out and touches him – so gently – on the shoulder. The focus pulls closer in.

It's Mel. Her face is small but unmistakeable. She reaches for something he's holding.

Kenneth paused the shot. Reclined. Exhaled.

'Funny looking cigarette that isn't it? Looks a bit big. Almost like one of Junie's.'

Mel tried to speak and failed.

'"Social Worker: My Drugs And Sex Shame."' Kenneth said. 'Make a good front page, don't you think, with the picture and all?'

'You…'

She couldn't complete the thought: you… you've been following me, or someone has, you secretly filmed me, you're… The car that was failing to start outside her window. She'd heard the sound before.

'So Kenneth,' she said, in a bright aggressive voice, 'so this is what, this is more blackmail?'

'Looks a bit funny though. Wouldn't you say? I mean, after all he is your – , what's your word for people like us…?'

'Client. He's my client.'

'That's it, client, and then blind me if he doesn't turn up, stark-bollock naked, in your gaff, and oh look, there you are as well, all friendly like, having a nice bit of kif… Well. What would you think? If you were your boss? On the basis of that piece of evidence I mean? Taking everything rationally…?'

'Kenneth I can't believe… I can't believe…' Mel was so angry that she lost momentarily the power of organised thought and merely stood, air seething around her face like moths. 'Kenneth. You didn't honestly think you were going to get away with this did you?'

'Everything's arranged. Dane will be taken care of, Kelly and me will marry, and Kelly will dance for me, as is customary. Today as it goes. June says the omens are very good. And she should know. She knows her omens does Junie.'

Mel was still and cold with rage. Her voice was far from what she would have liked it to be. She was dimly aware of the crowding and hissing and pounding of blood behind her ears. 'Must have been a bit of a setback then, me turning up when I did?' she said, and folded her arms in a way that, she knew, she could not possibly maintain for more than a minute.

'Not really. It's all a question of – discretion. Wouldn't you say?'

'And you think you've managed me do you Kenneth?'

He smiled that smile again, and Mel abruptly realised that she was either going to leave immediately or fucking land him a good one on his stupid fat smug fucking… She gathered control of herself again. Deep breaths. Her voice came out clear and authoritative.

'Kenneth, I'll tell you what's going to happen. I want Kelly back in school, not married to you, and not dancing. I want June to go back part-time to the launderette, after you and I have got rid of Boney by holding an exorcism…'

'Sorry love, a…?'

'You heard me. As for you, I want you to stop being the King of Cornwall in exile, Kenneth. I want you living somewhere else, away from Kelly. You will get over your bad back and your depression and do a diploma in IT or set up a market stall, and God damn it you will chair meetings of the Residents' Association. There will be no more holes, ever. I want the twins to stop doing rule of silence. And I want Dane…'

'Yeah I kind of guessed that already…'

'…to go back to Cornwall and finish his NVQ in food hygiene or whatever it is.'

'Don't want much do you? Well I would just like to wish you the best of luck with that my love. Now if you'll excuse me, I need to get changed. I've got a big day.'

'Kenneth...'

He lifted a finger, indicated the garden outside: 'Shhhhhhh. Can you not hear?'

'Kenneth, I'm hardly going to fall for that now am I...'

'Shhhhh, though.'

And, come to mention it, was there not some sound out there? Voices, and bizarrely could she not hear a horse somewhere nearby? Mel froze.

'Hadn't you better go and take a look?' he said.

Abruptly, with no warning, Mel realised that she had had enough. Kenneth's smug face was gleaming up out of the darkness at her intolerably, and, without any premeditation or consideration for the consequences of her actions or anything like that, she grabbed the sword from his feet and tore the velvet off. Kenneth stood furiously, but she poked the sword at him, almost playfully.

'My. Sharp, isn't it?' she said, running a finger along the edge. She began to untwist the leather binding. He took a step towards her, she danced backwards. Stalemate.

'You better not...' Kenneth started to say, but she shushed him, still pointing the dagger at him. The leather binding was free, and she could finally see the engraving on the blade clear and straight:

Warrior – Legends in Steel since 1974 – Sheffield Made.

She held Kenneth's eye.

'Oh now isn't that interesting Kenneth? See, I think everyone out there believes that the sword is – what was your word again? – Mesolithic, wasn't that it? Or Saxon maybe? Handed down from generation to generation, father to son, until exile ends? Something like that?'

'You…'

'You stay right here, Mister. You stay right here and don't make any fuss, or I will be showing each and every person out there the evidence…'

'You…'

'… the evidence, Kenneth, that you are not who you say you are, that the sword of kingship is in fact a piece of tourist tat, and that the wedding, regrettably, is off.' She moved closer to him with the dagger, allowed it to play along his bristly throat. He watched her, silent, with the same mocking expression. She felt a little thrill of power. She tore the videotape out of the machine and unravelled it, tying Kenneth to the chair, though not perhaps very permanently.

'Mind my bad back, now, won't you love?' Kenneth said, and Mel glared at him – this isn't over yet – and backed out into the garden. The key was in the padlock, and she guessed it would take Kenneth at least five minutes to break out. He was immediately hammering and calling for Paulie.

Night was ending over Whitehawk, grey rags of cloud and distraught seagulls wheeling overhead, portending disaster and disgrace. She met the beady determined eyes in front of her.

'You.'

39

Mrs. Slight was dressed in silver and grey, with a large dress hat, and seemed surprised and not particularly pleased to see Mel.

'Gracious, how you do show up everywhere!' she said, and made to brush her aside.

'Mrs. Slight,' Mel said, pulling at her sleeve, 'Do you know where Kelly is? I'm rather worried that she might…' she said, and stopped, as other figures appeared behind her, entering the back garden; June, Theresa, and, walking unsteadily between them, Kelly, magnificent, astonishing in the Adidas-stripes wedding dress, now complete with veiled baseball hat and high-heeled trainers. June, Mel noted, was out of doors for the first time since the Mentorn Hotel meeting. She had presumably been needed to dress Kelly at Theresa's. She now ducked frantically back into the house, pausing only for a second to consider the smashed back door. The sanctuary of the kitchen regained, she concentrated on giving Mel the evil eye.

'Kelly?' Mel said gently.

Kelly's head appeared to be not working quite properly: she lifted it, her eyes found Mel, but it fell back again, as if it was too heavy.

Mel looked from Kelly to Theresa, as more figures appeared in the entryway to the back garden. Mel was distracted again by the sound of animals, the jingling of metal, the creak of leather. Over the fence she could make out a large dark carriage parked outside the house, with two vast incongruous horses at the front. This, clearly, was a wedding on some scale.

Mel turned back to the garden, where Kenneth was thumping and banging in the shed, freeing himself from the videotape. She probably had no more than a few minutes before he got loose. She could make out the dim forms of people arriving through the back gate; Paulie, his ten-year old, a woman Mel didn't recognise. Mel, with a qualm of panic, realised that she was now effectively trapped between these two advancing parties. If she could just get hold of Kelly...

40

Jamie woke alone, suddenly, with a feeling of catastrophe ringing in his ears. The remnants of a dream were still reverberating in his head, deafening music that seemed to have no way of ending. He had been turning to the person sitting next to him and shouting into his ear, God I can't believe how long this all goes on for and nobody moves, when he woke up...

Mel was nowhere near, nor was her side of the bed warm. He squinted and blinked at the clock: five fifteen. Hardly time (yet) to get up and grapple with despair (again). Without fully intending to – without actually deciding to, in fact without ever having first become conscious that he was going to – he reached for the dog end of a joint lying irresistibly on the bedside table and sparked it up.

Light seeped in through the curtains, smoke billowed around him luxuriously. He finished the dog end and, because Mel wasn't there, felt no inhibition in screwing up the roach in his hand and dropping it into the murky region behind the headboard, instead of responsibly going and flushing it down the toilet (this was a non-smoking environment). He pounded out to the bathroom and stopped dead.

'Hello?'

Through the open front room door Jamie could make out the figure of Dane, in his pomp, at full stretch on the sofa, telly flickering, sound low. Mel's bloke, he remembered in a flash. The client: Approach With Caution.

'Hello? Still here then?' Jamie shouted from the hall. He hunted about for the name, but it wasn't coming.

Dane craned his head round, raised indifferent eyebrows as a greeting, and turned his attention back to the telly, which showed a smiling caramel-coloured woman in a low-cut cerise blouse waving her beautiful hands over a map of Britain. Dane was sitting up with the duvet round his middle, wreathed in a smoke fug of his own. Ashtray at elbow. Cosy.

'Where's Mel?' Jamie said, not wishing it to sound quite so much like an accusation.

'She'll be here any time. She's gone to get Kelly. In a ship.' Dane said, barely interested.

'A ship. Really.'

Dane nodded, eyes still fixed on the telly. Jamie considered him, assessing menace, craziness, etc. Client, he thought. Jesus, he's a client. It could mean almost anything: normally though they didn't get through the front door. He ducked into the kitchen and rang Mel, but it went straight to answering machine. He returned to the front room door and regarded Dane again.

'Well. I've got to be out of here in forty five minutes or so,' he said, 'so I'm afraid I'm going to have to ask you...'

'Yeah no worries. Don't mind me.'

'No I mean, you'd better leave with me.'

'Why? Where are we going?'

'I mean I don't want you here unattended,' Jamie said, point blank, and Dane craned his neck round with merry curiosity.

'Yeah? Don't you? Only I got to wait here see for Kelly to come. Won't be long now.'

'In a ship.'

Slow nodding. Jamie felt that he was failing to get his message across.

'See, she was going to marry my Uncle Marke. Thinks he's King of Cornwall in exile or summat. Right. June Ireland, who, incidentally, is a fat slag, promised him Kelly.'

'When you say "promised"…?'

'He's going to marry her. It's a dynastic thing. Yeah right. And I was supposed to give her away, cos her dad's, you know, busy at the moment.'

'I see,' Jamie said softly, 'OK.' He was having trouble following this. All he had really registered so far was, why "Mark-e"? I mean, why?

'But see, she give me something didn't she? Kelly? Herbal tea. And now…'

'Now…' Jamie prompted.

'Well. I've only gone and fallen for her myself haven't I? Kenneth finds out doesn't he, gets that cunt Paulie onto me with a fucking big knife right…' Dane put his head in his hands and howled, suddenly and hard, making Jamie break out in sweat. 'So I had to come here. She'll come for me here. Oh Christ. I've only gone and done it now haven't I? Trust me. Trust stupid – bloody – me…' Dane was banging his head into his knuckles.

Jamie had a panicky feeling that he should try to offer solace of some kind; but didn't. He suddenly felt an irresistible urge to skin up and, sitting in the other chair, did that instead.

'I see,' he said, some distant recollection of Mel's professional manner coming to him from afar. 'Yes. OK.'

King promised virgin – King's nephew falls for her instead – all ends very very badly. Lots of love and death. Jamie blinked the thought away, but it returned.

'Wait a minute.' He held his hand up, unnoticed by Dane

who was still sobbing lustily while manicured weather came from the west, guided on by softly waving caramel-coloured hands. But a thought was coming to him, something familiar but long ago, something to do with singing. He frowned down at it. The joint lay unmade on his knee.

'No wait.'

King of Cornwall is promised Irish Princess, who is young virgin. She is delivered to him…

'…on a ship…'

by King's nephew, but she gives nephew a love potion and

'…he falls for her. He falls in love with her…'

but they cannot be together, they fear the wrath of King…
…Marke.

so Nephew, wounded by King's man, retreats to his castle in…

Jamie sat, his hand still held up in a gesture of silence.

'You're having a laugh aren't you?' he said finally. Dane – clearly – was not. 'Well I tell you something, my friend,' Jamie said with some difficulty, 'I think there's something very odd going on here…'

41

Mel took a step towards Kelly, who was still being held up by Theresa. A strangled wail came from June from the kitchen.

'It's OK,' Mel said very softly. 'It's OK, Kelly.' Kelly was just beginning to let her droopy eyes open and focus on Mel when Mel's phone went off, vibrate and ring, appallingly loud and sudden. She wrestled it out of her jacket pocket. It was awkward, as she only had one hand free, the other still holding the dagger.

'Mel, hi it's me.'

'Yeah Jamie, I'm a bit busy at the moment,' she said, still judging distances and angles.

'Mel, I thought you should know something…'

'Yes?'

'Yeah, it's not going to be easy to explain actually…'

She sighed, decided to give him her attention.

'Is it about Dane? Is he OK?'

'Yeah, oh yeah, no it's not that. It's… Look. 1865. Munich. First performance of an opera, by Richard Wagner…'

'Yeah? Jamie, look, I really am quite busy at the moment…'

'…called Tristan and Isolde. Do you want to hear the story?'

'Not sure I've got time right now Jamie, kind of got my hands full, thanks though…'

'I think you should hear it. King Marke – Mar-kuh – of Cornwall is promised a young Irish Princess, who is brought to him by the King's nephew. His nephew.'

'Nephew. Got it.' She was only half-listening. 'Jamie, can I call you back...'

'Young Princess – Isolde – gives nephew – Tristan – a love potion. He falls in love with her. So instead of marrying old King Marke she has it away with the handsome Nephew. King Marke finds out...'

'What? Wait.' She held up a hand, though he wasn't there to see it, 'Jamie, what are you saying to me?'

'Your people. Your – your clients. They're acting it out. Tristan and Isolde. To the letter. They don't know they are, but they are. And it's spreading. OK, guess where nephew Tristan gets taken after he's wounded? Guess?'

'Don't know...'

'Brittany. His castle in Brittany.'

Brittany Road. Nah...

'He has a loyal servant, guess what his name is?'

'Don't know...'

'Kurwenal. What's my name, Mel?'

'Jamie. Kurwen.'

'Kurwen. Yeah.'

She stood and held the phone.

'But...'

But that just isn't reasonable, she was thinking, as music suddenly burst out of nowhere, a high female voice, lost in a swirling vapour of longing and abandon, unfolding, turning on the air. It seemed to be coming from every direction at once, echoing eerily across the valley, drifting from the sky, louder and louder, getting closer.

'Mel you still there? Dane's going completely ape, he's tearing his bandages off now...'

'Is that in the story?'

'Oh yeah. By the book. And he's off on the love and death as well. You should hear him.' Mel was indeed aware of a muffled commotion somewhere in the background, shouting and the overturning of furniture. Oh yeah, ships is it? I'll give you ships in a minute if you don't... Dane will you KEEP your fucking PANTS on, for fuck's... Mel shifted the phone to the other hand.

'And Jamie? Not that I'm saying you're necessarily right about this, but what actually, you know...' she glanced over at Kelly, a drugged teen bride slumped in Theresa's arms, 'what happens? In the end?'

'Well let's see now. Tristan waits for Isolde to come and join him in Brittany. He's pretty mad at this point. She arrives finally, and lo! they are together. Both, of course, immediately start obsessing about dying together...'

'How do you know these things Jamie?'

'Did it for A-level didn't I? I remember thinking at the time, in fact, hmm, here's a story that lacks what you might call...'

'Reasonableness?'

'Yeah. That. And now, apparently, it's landed.'

'As if it was in the air somehow? Like a cloud? But how is that possible...?' Mel was thinking of the hints and throbs and shocks of music she's been hearing, the longing, the throbbing, the...

'Mel? You still there?'

'Oh yeah Jamie, sorry...'

'Anyway, next, as I recall it, King Marke arrives. Tristan thinks he's come to get Isolde back from him, to separate them, and to kill Tristan. In fact, he's come to say that he's fine, actually, with the whole thing, he's forgiven Tristan, and they can get married if that's what they want...'

'But I'm guessing that's not actually what happens…'

'Nope. That would make way too much sense. No, instead Tristan dies in Isolde's arms, and then there's the most terrible lot of love and death, after which Isolde falls lifeless on Tristan's corpse in the time-honoured manner, her last words being "Rapture! Rapture!"…'

'Ah. Not good then. In social work terms, I mean. Rapture, that's rarely what we call an optimum outcome.'

'Oh and do you want to guess what happens to Kurwenal, incidentally?'

'It wouldn't involve heroic death would it?'

'If I were you, Mel, I would take some pains to make sure that Kelly doesn't make it over here today.'

'OK then. Great. Thanks Jamie,' Mel said. 'Not that I'm, you know, necessarily…'

She hung up on him. She wasn't saying he was right, of course not, but then again it did seem to account for the evidence in a way that she, frankly, couldn't otherwise do…

'Now Kelly?' She spoke quietly, calmly into Kelly's ear.

'Sod off you fat cow…'

It was true, she suddenly knew it with certainty. It was the only explanation that fitted all the evidence. And wasn't she committed to evidence-based decision making? The fact that it seemed, on the face of it, unlikely was neither here nor there… Her mind seemed to swim suddenly, to melt away, and she had to shake her head to clear her thoughts. She reached a decision.

'OK Kelly. No love and death for you young lady. We're calling a halt to this right now.' She grabbed hold of Kelly and pulled her to her body, the dagger menacing anyone who tried to interfere. 'It'll be fine. I know exactly what I'm doing now.'

The wedding guests had assembled into a single large group, standing about in the gathering light. June appeared at the kitchen door, dressed now in her cream and white tent, tugging at a shoulder strap. It occurred to Mel that they were all perhaps waiting for the exact moment. June's omens, she guessed, were specific as to time of day. Dawn, a likely candidate, could only be minutes away.

Mrs. Slight peeled herself away from the front of the crowd and stood, a small smartly-dressed woman, squaring up to her, the self-appointed ringleader. Mel was trying to hold Kelly behind her back, but Kelly was coming round now, and starting to take a somewhat more active interest in proceedings. Mel caught her by the wrist, tight.

'Mrs. Slight?' she said. 'How nice to…'

Mrs. Slight quivered in the uncertain light. Her voice was a hiss.

'This is her day. This is my day. You're not having her. You hear me?'

'Sorry,' Mel said, 'I'm not sure I…'

'I've put years into that girl.'

'Yes I believe so,' Mel said levelly. 'What, three lessons a week for six years, at, say, twenty quid a throw? That comes to, let's think now…'

Mrs. Slight stood her ground. 'This is hardly what I would call professional conduct…'

'That's if she was having lessons all of that time? I mean, it's not as if there's much to show for it is there? And who drove her to dance and back? Kenneth. Lots of time, with Kenneth, in a car. Alone. With your collusion.'

'Allegations, insinuations…'

'It was you that was following me, filming me. Wasn't it?'

'Kelly belongs here. She's ours, not yours. You can't take her. You've no right…'

'Mrs. Slight? Before we get into any further discussion of all this…' Mel said politely, and managed to short-circuit the debate that might have followed by punching her with her whole weight, full on the kisser. Bam! Lights out, sister. She went down like a sack of potatoes, Mel thought with satisfaction, and she wasn't getting up again in a hurry either. Mel licked her knuckles. Where reason had failed… She looked up and saw, gratifyingly if perhaps a little alarmingly, that every eye was now on her and her alone. The situation, she sensed, was growing more serious by the minute. She needed to reassert control. Mel raised her voice, her cool, assertive, commanding voice.

'Look everyone, could I have your attention a moment? Now what I'm about to say is going to sound… well, it's going to sound, how can I say…?'

She didn't get any further: Kelly, fighting off the last traces of the drug, shoved her violently in the face and took unsteadily off, her heels doing possibly irreparable damage to the already knackered grass, running for love and death and Dane. Mel rugby tackled her but came up with nothing but fistfuls of polyester train. Kelly was gone.

Mel turned back to the wedding party.

'Right then.' She held the sword aloft, waving it about so that everyone could see. It was surprisingly light. 'OK everyone. You know what, I've about had enough. I'm going to go and get Kelly now and put a stop to all this once and for all. And if anyone would care to try to stop me…?' She gestured with the dagger. 'Anyone? Mrs. Slight? Or Paulie maybe? Can't tempt you?' She backed out of the garden and down the passage, the dagger glinting in the gathering light. The wedding crowd followed, warily, watchfully: it was a kind of slow motion chase. Mel kept the sword held high until she reached the safety of her car.

She became aware she was being followed after about five minutes. There was a familiar sound of a gearbox crunching, and there it was in her rear view mirror, Mrs. Slight's trusty Volvo. She could make out Paulie in the passenger seat, with Kenneth, freed now from his bondage, dimly visible in the back. I am not breaking any traffic laws for these people she stated firmly to herself, but found that her driving was becoming ever more enthusiastic anyway. There was no traffic about at this hour. Just as well.

She rang Jamie.

'Any sign of Kelly?'

'I guess you mean the foul-mouthed pre-teen in the wedding dress?'

'That'll be her. So, anyone dead yet?'

'Not quite yet.'

'I did try to stop her getting there…'

'Well you failed and so now we're into Act Three, Mel.'

'I'm on my way, Jamie. Just try to make sure no one dies or anything before I get there. OK?'

'Now why didn't I think of that?' Jamie said.

'So what is it exactly that comes next?'

'Well, what we're waiting for now is for Melot to arrive, with King Marke. Melot is his trusted…'

'What? Melot? Mel-ot?'

'Oh did I not mention Melot before?'

'Jamie… you don't think that could, by any chance, be me, do you?

'Hmmmm…'

'What does he do?'

'He kills Tristan in a fight…'

'Oh brilliant.'

'Look Mel, you'll be fine as long as you don't kill Dane.'

'I'll try to remember that Jamie. I'll make a note to self…'

She parked badly and, grabbing the dagger, barged up the stairs to the flat.

'Jamie?'

Inside, there was so much confusion that she barely knew where to start. Kelly was making the most noise, emitting a series of shrieks and deprecations that were, surely, in breach of noise restrictions, while Dane, largely naked, was bellowing away back at her, as he messed with his bandages. 'I wasn't on a fucking ship, you dickhead!' Kelly was screaming, as Jamie hid in the kitchen, with his head in his hands.

Mel, still full of the rather delightful power that possession of a big, nasty-looking dagger was investing her with, decided to start with Kelly, purely for the noise reduction value. She grabbed her and managed to get part of a cushion into her mouth, tying her arms behind her with the torn sleeve of the dress. The shrieking was muffled, but showed no sign of stopping. Dane lunged towards them, but Mel held Kelly in front of her and backed away, into the hallway. She was aware of noise from the street, cars and men and shouting.

'It's OK Kelly,' she murmured into her ear, as she and Dane postured awkwardly for position. Mel's arm was tiring from holding the dagger out. She dropped Kelly, who thrashed impotently on the floor, trying to get free of the polyester cocoon. Dane was approaching, lumbering towards her, the bandages unravelling round his leg.

'Dane. OK. Now wait just a moment…'

'Who dares his life against mine?'

'Yes Dane, that's a good point, of course, but if I could just direct your attention to the dagger for a moment, the so-called...'

She was aware of the sound of the front door breaking, banging and thumping as people surged up the stairs.

'Defend yourself!' Dane called out.

'Dane? Now I know this may not be the best time to mention it, but if you wouldn't mind just taking a look at this?' She held the dagger out sideways, still holding it, angling the blade so he could read the inscription. Dane didn't look as if he was taking much in, he looked drugged and blurry, intent on just one thing, the figure of Kelly slumped behind Mel. Mel raised her voice. 'Dane, think about it for a moment. I mean, what sense does any of this make? If I could just appeal to your unusually high aggregate rationality index... I mean your Kui/Varney scores were... Dane, just look at this for a minute will you, it's clear evidence that...'

Quite how it happened she would often ponder in the years to come, and the board of enquiry would subsequently acquit of her of any intentional action, but Dane suddenly was on top of her, on top of the dagger, he was looking straight into her eyes for a long slow moment, as a jolt of music crashed over her, no delicate throbbing now but a terrible thrashing assault, strings fighting and spiralling, up and up and up, demented with longing and abandon, it was like the waves, coming and coming, crashing and battering, the sky was full of it. She saw Dane, slick with sweat, face contorted, wracked and shuddering in slow spurts of ecstasy, rapture! Rapture! She banged her hands to her ears and as suddenly it was all gone again, as if the wind had shifted. Just a high ringing in the ears, like a vibration.

'Fuck me girl, you don't piss about do you…' Dane slurred, and slumped to the floor, blood pooling around him. The dagger slid back out of his body as he fell, and Mel regarded it as it dripped slow viscid blood onto the butterscotch carpet, as the door to the flat was broken down and Kenneth and Paulie swarmed in, followed by Mrs. Slight. They came to a seething standstill in front of Mel, who lifted the dripping dagger aloft and seemed to be about to say something.

'Everyone? OK, what I thought we might do is have an unscheduled family conference. You see, I think I've finally got it now…' she was shouting, when she heard an entirely unexpected sound, from the front door: a polite male voice.

'Mel?'

December

42

'Is she here now?' said the woman standing next to Mel, waving her glass around.

'Someone said she was in the building somewhere. They saw her security going in half an hour ago,' Mel said distantly.

Cherie Blair. In person. The glamorous wife of the dashing Prime Minister himself, and public advocate of rationality targets. Thirty-eight of the pilot scheme staff, Mel included, had been invited to an afternoon drinks party, at a function room at the Office of the Deputy Prime Minister, with Cherie-Blair-no-less as guest speaker. Lofty ceilings, creamy white walls and fabulously well-polished doors, every bit as shiny as they were on the telly, Mel thought. Burly men in suits muttering into shoulder mics. Everybody security-tagged and patted down. Everybody on edge.

'I could hardly sleep last night,' the woman said, glancing twitchily round as she spoke, and Mel turned full face to her. Mel was feeling the effects of some considerable medication (diazepam), given to her by an RU medic when she had explained to him about being followed, spied on, seduced by the music, and how everything would be fine as soon as June's herbal tea had stopped working on her. The medication was lovely, she was cool, she was calm, she was a touch dry-mouthed. But not twitchy, she thought, sllooowly. No siiir. She felt detached, amused, not-here. She smiled at the woman beside her. Poor love, she thought. Ah you poor, poor love.

'Why not? Why couldn't you sleep?'

The woman – Mel couldn't focus sufficiently well to read her name tag – gave her a shocked look.

'Cherie Blair!' she said, and Mel shrugged.

'Oh. That.'

Mel's speech – no more than two minutes long; there was a great deal of business to get through, and Cherie Blair had to be across London at the opening of a new type of junior school at 2.30pm – had been through some changes.

Thoroughly vetted by a brisk young woman from the Office of the Deputy Prime Minister Communications Team, neatly printed out on five pieces of paper and now folded up in the breast pocket of her jacket, it was a winning account of perseverance and determination, with a paragraph at the end looking forward to a day when every local authority in the country had its own Rationality Unit team. Her original speech had been largely edited out. Snip snip snip, as the Communications Team woman had said. 'I'm wondering if we really need all this... bottom of page two through to, say, middle of six?'

'About Tristan...'

'Yes...'

'And about them following me, spying on me? And the accident? You see, all I was trying to do was show him the dagger...'

'Yes. All that. To be honest, I think it just muddles your message.' The woman was in her last month in the post, before moving onwards and upwards to a PR job with a think tank. 'Accuracy, brevity, clarity: abc = impact! Snip snip snip. Now this I like. Middle page seven?'

'The test scores? But...'

'Yes. Now this I can really hear you saying. This is good.'

'Ladies and gentlemen,' she said in her head, 'it is with tremendous pride that I am standing here today...'

(June sits smoking at the window of the launderette at the bottom of Whitehawk Way as the winter light fades. From far away comes the howling of a dog; she puts her head out of the door, sniffs the wind; an exorcism, she knows, just moves a restless spirit from one place to another. Boney, she is certain, is still here, somewhere, snuffling his ghostly way round the back-entries and twittens of Whitehawk... She stiffens, shivers, pulls her cardigan tighter around her. It'll get worse...)

When Mel had heard herself being addressed, by name, in the flat, as Dane bled at her feet, she had assumed she was in trouble. Big trouble. Things, after all, could have been seen to be going not all that well at that moment, she reflected. She could certainly see how someone might assess her as having further training and supervision needs, what with the attempted forcible abduction of child brides, stabbing of clients and so on. She could see how it might all look, from the outside.

'Mel?'

It had been Richard, the supervisor, in a beatific haze of jasmine and sandalwood. Behind him Mel could see two men dressed in paramilitary outfits, boots and protective vests. On their shoulders, the distinctive black and white RU logo.

'I can explain everything,' she'd started weakly, but Richard had interrupted.

'Mel? We are enormously pleased to be able to tell you that you have exceeded every target the ODPM, the RU and indeed the whole EU Reason Directorate have set. Your last batch of score results... well, they are enormously impressive and you are to be congratulated. In fact, we are able to confirm – confidentially, mind – that you will be approached by officials at the ODPM – the DPM, I understand, is taking a particular interest in this – '

'DPM?' Mel said. She could feel her sense of reality wandering slightly. She had a bitter taste in her mouth, and the seagulls kept screaming at her. 'Sorry, Richard, would you say that again?'

'Deputy Prime Minister. There's a feeling that we need to broadcast these achievements more widely, get some press, really blow our own trumpets.'

'Great,' Mel said, and, carefully helped Kelly stand up. 'I do hope you won't think me rude,' Mel said, hoisting her onto her shoulder, 'but I do really have to deal with this. See, she can't go back home because she's twelve and her stepfather plans to marry her, today as it turns out, because of the omens. Obviously it's no good here either, because, since she gave Dane the love potion... Well, you know... Oh we're going to need an ambulance of course, for Dane. I think that would be best practice anyway, Richard, don't you? But if she goes with him, then it'll all be love and death and rapture and so on and I really don't see that as a desirable outcome here. So I think she's probably going to have to live in my car for a while.'

'Not living in your frigging fat car, you gay bitch...' Kelly managed to slur.

'You see,' Mel explained confidentially to Richard, his glasses glinting, 'they're acting out Tristan and Isolde. Of course, they don't know they are...'

'Yes. Well we can talk about that in due course. But as of now, this project is terminated.'

'But you can't...'

'Protocol 12/6?'

'Remind me, Richard.'

'"The Rationality Unit Directorate will have complete discretion with regard to duration of projects. Where an RU decision is taken to decommission an operation, the Field Operative will offer an immediate cessation of responsibility and will make available to authorised RU personnel all logs, reports, data, test scores and other..."'

'But Richard I was just about to chair a family meeting. You see, I've found it, the Master Theme. I finally...'

'That's alright Mel. We'll take care of it from here.'

'You're going to send me back to Child and Family,' she said bitterly, 'aren't you?' She was still holding Kelly in front of her, and noticed how, from one point of view, it could almost look as if she was using her as a hostage.

'Mel.' Richard made a tiny, almost imperceptible crease between his eyebrows appear and then vanish again. It meant: let go of the girl, and put down the dagger.

'Look Richard, if this is about the bonfire being too close to the house...'

Richard indicated no.

'Then why? Why now? When I understand them?'

'This project has been successfully implemented. You are invited to leave the scene and make yourself available for debriefing.'

He motioned to her to release Kelly. She was torn, but she had no other options now. She let go. Kelly took a few stumbling steps towards him, turned her head back at Mel.

'Go with him,' Mel said. 'It's for the best now. All of you,' she called out as the RU muscle prised the dagger from her gory fist and ushered her away, 'you can do any mad thing you like now. Marry the fucking dog for all I care. I've done all I can.' She felt tears stinging her eyes as she was assisted into the waiting car. 'I did all I could, I did,' she pleaded, and was answered by a stolid silence from the two men in the front, as the flat was flooded with uniformed RU troops, quarantining and securing and generally locking down the situation, whilst Richard handed out user satisfaction questionnaires to the uncomprehending family. It was over.

(Kelly is in school, writing a poem about snow. Snow is like wool coming out of the sky. Snow is, like, really wet on my eye. She sighs. Her paper is more doodling than actual writing. Elaborated letter D's. She is a heavier figure now than in the summer, the antidepressants are taking their toll on her. Dane is lurking in his Audi, waiting for her, just at the limits of his Anti Social Behaviour Order exclusion zone. He's not scared of Kenneth. He's just got to keep his eyes open. Like, all the time.)

Back at the reception Mel was waiting to go on. 'Ladies and gentlemen…' Her speech told of how she had met targets brilliantly, she had exceeded targets, she had, in short, fucked targets up the ass! No but seriously folks. She gathered her face. No, really. No smiling.

She went on to express optimism about the national roll-out, planned to begin as soon as parliamentary time could be found to push it through. Certainly next session, an ODPM spokesman had said recently on Newsnight, or perhaps the session after that. But definitely, if not this parliamentary term, then just as soon as anything. And that, he said, was a commitment. And reports of unusually high levels of drop out amongst staff? High levels of stress-related illness? Concerns that pilot scheme staff members had been intimidated, threatened, and clients injured? He had instigated a thorough enquiry.

Words slurred lazily through her mind, she lost her balance for a second, and then became aware of a guiding hand on her elbow.

'Ms. Banff? You'll be on in about five minutes. We thought you might like to actually make an entrance rather than just shuffle on…'

(Two weeks ago Mel had been sent, anonymously, wedding pictures of Kenneth and a groggy-looking Kelly. Along with the pictures was something wrapped in plastic: she had screamed and dropped it at the first touch: Jamie had come running in and, after some careful scrutiny, declared it to be the tongue of a dog.

Kenneth is digging in the garden at his brother's house in Cornwall, arranging further assaults on Dane and Gary Chope with Paulie by text message. Gary Chope, his nose repaired now with a plastic prosthetic that glues on, is on the train to Truro, a stolen gun snug in his jacket pocket, having got the address from June. Kenneth's tenure as King of Cornwall (in exile) is about to come to an abrupt end…)

Mel was led away by security to an area behind the screens and cameras and lights. The screens were emblazoned with the Thinking it Through logo, alongside other fainter overlapping words in various sizes of lower case, words like 'empowering' and 'independent'. Mel slid the papers from her pocket and awaited her cue. She was not, she thought, nervous at all. The thought surprised and amused her slightly.

'Ms. Banff? OK. They're ready for you.' She heard an announcement and some silence, then a slow round of scattered applause. She heard her name being called. More applause. She aimed herself at the softly swaying podium.

'Lazheeez and gennnemen...'

Three minutes later it was all over. Mel was given a few seconds of subdued applause, and some camera flashes went off. There was a gesture at her elbow, and she was led gently off the podium and away. She struggled for a moment, she even appeared to be trying to say something, but was guided to a private area with chairs and security guards, where she found Jamie, and sat and waited for Cherie Blair.

The End